degrees betrayal

sierra's story
{DANDI DALEY MACKALL}

ryun's story
{JEFF NESBIT}

kenzie's story
{MELODY CARLSON}

{kenzie's story}

{kenzie's story}

degrees OF betrAIal

MELODY CARLSON

thirsty

Tyndale House Publishers, Inc.
Wheaton, Illinois

Go to Degreesofbetrayal.com or areUthirsty.com for more info.

thirsty(?) is a trademark of Tyndale House Publishers, Inc.

Designed by Julie Chen

Library of Congress Cataloging-in-Publication Data

Carlson, Melody.
   Kenzie's story / Melody Carlson.
      p. cm. — (Degrees of betrayal)
   Summary: Finally part of the popular crowd, Kenzie begins spending too much money
on clothes, avoiding church, and dating her best friend's boyfriend behind her back, but
a serious car accident and its aftermath force her to make things right with her friends,
and with God.
   ISBN 1-4143-0002-6 (sc)
[1. Popularity—Fiction.   2. Interpersonal relations—Fiction.   3. High schools—Fiction.
4. Conduct of life—Fiction.   5. Traffic accidents—Fiction.   6. Schools—Fiction.]
I. Title. II. Series.
   PZ7.C216637Ke 2004
   [Fic]—dc22   2004003694

Printed in the United States of America

08 07 06 05 04
 7   6   5   4   3   2   1

I hadn't always wished I was someone else. But that day I did. I'd have given almost anything to be like those *other* girls. You know the ones I mean—they laugh loudly and cut up (among themselves) and their hair is always perfect and their teeth are straight and white and they dress like they just stepped off the slick pages of *In Style* or *Glamour* or *Seventeen*.

On most days I was perfectly happy with who I was and how I looked. My best friend, Anna Krenshaw, even thought I was pretty. And most of the time I thought I had it basically together. But there were moments I wanted to be someone else. Like someone who was as cool and together as, say, Sierra Reynolds.

But the main reason I felt like that was because

of this one particular guy. A guy who, in my opinion, was the coolest guy at Highview High, maybe even the coolest guy on the planet. His name was Ryun Lee and right then he was dribbling the ball downfield, getting ready to make another spectacular goal.

I'd been in love with Ryun for a long time At least most of my junior year. Everything about him seemed so perfect. But, unfortunately, he didn't even know that I existed. Not yet anyway.

The good news was that Ryun did NOT have a girlfriend yet either. And that day I'd come to school with a plan, thinking that maybe, just maybe, I might be able to get this guy to speak to me. I knew that meant I had to say something to him first—and hopefully something intelligent. And since I'd been a faithful fan at every single one of his soccer matches, and since I'd studied every single move he made on the field, and since I understood soccer pretty well (I used to be pretty good before I broke my ankle my freshman year) I was thinking that maybe, just maybe, I could come up with something halfway decent to say. I even had on a new Lucky sweatshirt and my best jeans and, although I wasn't an expert on those things, I thought I looked fairly decent. Or at least okay.

That was until I noticed the "cool girls" hanging over by the bleachers. Then I wasn't so sure anymore. I wasn't blind. I could see the way Ryun glanced their way from time to time. And I could tell he *cared* about what they thought.

But he didn't even seem to notice Anna or me.

He didn't seem to hear us yelling for him to steal the ball and cheering for him when he scored a goal. He didn't seem to know that we'd come to every one of his games, even when it was cold and raining. No, he just raced past us like we were invisible.

I guess I'd describe us as "fringers" since we stayed along the edges of things. I mean, we *knew* the kids who were popular and had brief conversations with them, but for the most part we were outside the elite crowd.

Still, I'd been pretty much okay with that. I had my music and art, plus youth group and my job at the day-care center at our church. And I made good grades and got along well with others. I should have been perfectly happy, right?

So, what was wrong? Okay, I admit it. Sometimes I was jealous of girls like Sierra and her everpopular friends. *And especially that day.* But it seemed like they had more than their fair share of the fun.

It didn't help that Sierra was petite and had gorgeous auburn hair and emerald green eyes. Her dad had this big psychiatric practice in town. I could tell by the way Sierra dressed that they were loaded. She always made High High's best-dressed list in the newspaper. (I happened to think that list was lame, not to mention insulting to the rest of us.) Fortunately they didn't have a worst-dressed list or my name would have been a regular there.

I knew I was having a bad attitude that day and I should have put those negative thoughts out of my head and enjoyed the sunshine, the soccer match, and my good friend Anna's company . . . *but I just couldn't!*

Sometimes I convinced myself that Sierra and her crowd were all shallow and boring and not even worth knowing. But other times I found myself looking longingly at them and wishing I could be like them. Anna knew—she just sensed it sometimes. "Why are you even looking at them?" she asked me, as she caught me glancing their way again. Of course, I was only looking because *Ryun* was looking. I was wondering which one of those girls was capturing his attention and why.

"Huh?" I turned my attention to Anna.

"You know what I mean," she said. "It's so obvious. It's like you wish you could be part of their group, Kenzie."

"I do not."

She laughed. "You should see your face right now."

"Whatever." I focused my eyes back on the soccer field. The match had ended, and my big moment was almost here. "I'll be right back, Anna," I said quickly as I headed over to where Ryun was being congratulated by his teammates. I edged closer and watched for the moment he broke away from his soccer buddies. Then I walked over to him and waved. He had a funny expression, like he was trying to remember whether he knew me or not.

"Nice game, Ryun," I said in a controlled voice, acting all cool and composed, like my knees weren't turning into wet noodles.

He smiled. Gorgeous smile, by the way. "Thanks."

"That last goal was a perfect setup," I continued, not wanting to let him or that moment get away too soon.

"Huh?" His brow creased, as if he doubted I knew what I was talking about.

"It was calm," I said, wishing I felt that way myself. "That move with the outside of your left foot."

He really took a second look at me. "Huh? You saw that?"

"Sure." I nodded. "The keeper thought you were going to the left. Taking it right like that took him completely by surprise." I managed to say a few more intelligent-sounding things about the game, and he actually seemed to be listening. Suddenly I was feeling seriously hopeful. Maybe my eight years of playing soccer weren't a total waste.

But then Sierra Reynolds came along, and Ryun's gaze moved quickly from me to her. I could tell he was studying her with hungry eyes, like he couldn't get enough of this girl who looked like an ad for some big name designer. I stared down at the grass beneath my scuffed-up Birkenstock sandals and realized I was way out of my league, over my head, biting off more than I could chew—just pick the cliché and it would work.

I walked back to Anna, feeling like a total loser.

"What was up with that?" she asked, obviously curious about my stupid move on Ryun.

"Nothing," I said. "Let's get out of here."

"But what were you doing?"

"Trying to compete with Miss Fashion Queen." I shook my head as we walked away. "Can you imagine how much someone like Sierra must spend on clothing, Anna? Her shoes alone probably cost more than my whole outfit, including my backpack."

"I just don't get why you care so much about those airheads," she said.

"Airheads?" I paused to study my friend. She wasn't usually so critical of people, even if she didn't like them.

She shrugged. "Well, you know . . ."

"I *don't* care about them." I tried to convince her as we approached the parking lot.

"Then why are you talking about them right now?"

I studied Anna for a minute. She had been my best friend for years, and you couldn't ask for a better friend. Anna was loyal and intelligent and even quite pretty, not to mention she dressed better than I did. Anna was Chinese by birth. She had been abandoned as a baby, then rescued by an adoption agency and later placed with an older couple in our church. Her life had had some tough challenges, but all things considered, it seemed to be going pretty well to me. She was an only child, and she usually got whatever she wanted. So in some ways she wasn't much different than girls like Sierra and her friends. Only, of course, Anna was much nicer, and she was my friend.

"You want my honest answer?" I asked her as we approached her car.

"Yeah." She eyed me curiously as she fished her keys from her purse.

"The thing is, Anna, it's just *not* fair."

Anna frowned at me as she tossed her shiny black hair over her shoulder. "Well, get used to it, Kenzie," she said in a matter-of-fact voice. "Because life's not always fair."

"I know," I admitted. "But it just figures—the first time Ryun Lee has an actual conversation with me, Sierra has to come along and steal the show!"

"What did you expect, Kenzie?" Anna rolled her eyes at me. "Did you really think that Ryun Lee, the soccer king, was going to ask you out or something?"

"Well, nooo . . ."

"Really, Kenzie," she said as she unlocked her car, "it's not worth beating yourself up for him."

"How do you know?" I slumped down into the passenger seat of her immaculate Nissan, a gift for her 17th birthday a few months ago, and sighed deeply.

"Well, why would he blow you off for Sierra if he was?" She turned on the ignition and backed up.

"Yeah, you're probably right." I leaned back and closed my eyes, hoping that my agreeing with her would end this stupid conversation. But even with my eyes closed, all I could see was Ryun. The way he ran down the field with such incredible skill and speed. His long tan legs and the way he gave his head a shake after shooting a tricky goal . . . I'd never say such a lame thing out loud, but Ryun Lee was like poetry in motion. Truly beautiful. And talk about ripped. I was sure that guy had muscles over every inch of his body.

I knew that Ryun was Korean and that his father

ran a bunch of grocery stores around town. I knew he drove a dark blue Explorer that always looked clean and shiny and that he made good grades, although I wasn't sure why he hadn't joined Honor Society yet. I also knew he was getting all kinds of offers for college scholarships and some of them were quite impressive. But that was about all I knew about him.

Ryun Lee seemed to be the kind of guy who kept mostly to himself. But even that made him appealing to me—kind of mysterious and intriguing. And until that thing happened with Sierra, I'd imagined that Ryun might have room in his life for someone like me. I felt that we were alike, simpatico, you know. Don't ask me why, because I couldn't explain it in a thousand years. But I just had this feeling that he and I could have something, if I ever got the chance. For starters, there was soccer. I'd always loved soccer and would still be playing if I hadn't been injured. But breaking my ankle and missing an entire soccer season really set me back. Then my ankle never healed up as strong as it had once been.

At the time I told myself it was a blessing in disguise since not playing soccer had given me time to take up the guitar, get interested in art, and begin working more hours at the day care. But I still missed the thrill of the game. And watching Ryun Lee play was the next best thing.

I peeked over at Anna as she turned her car down the street to the day-care center where I worked. She'd been pretty quiet. I felt guilty for shutting her down, but it was obvious she didn't understand my attraction for Ryun. She'd probably just laugh if I told her about how I had gotten up that very morning with my big plan for winning him over after the match today. Why shouldn't she laugh? And besides, even if I did manage to catch him, how could I possibly keep him?

The one thing you can say about life is that it's almost always unexpected. And just as I was harboring a serious grudge against Sierra Reynolds, a surprising thing happened.

"Hey, Kenzie," Sierra called out to me one day in late April of our junior year. "Got a minute?"

I shrugged and walked cautiously toward her. Sierra and her friends might be snobs, but they weren't mean, at least not the way I knew some girls could be. Still, you wanted to watch your step around them. "What's up?" I asked.

"You're into art, aren't you?"

I shrugged again. "I guess so."

"She's really good," said Holly with a bright smile. "You should see the mural she painted at Little Lambs."

"Little Lambs?" echoed Sierra.

"It's a day-care center that Kenzie's mom runs at our church," said Holly. "And Kenzie did this totally awesome mural with trees and flowers and animals and a rainbow and, well, the kids really love it."

I relaxed. "Thanks," I told her.

"Great," said Sierra. "You're just what we need."

"Huh?"

"For the yearbook committee," Sierra said calmly, like she had the world in control. And she always did.

"Isn't it kind of late for that?" I asked.

"Not really. We're just doing layout now, and we've got some good photographers, but no one has a really good artistic eye. Do you think you could give us a hand?"

"I—uh—I guess so," I stammered. As if anyone could ever turn Sierra down for anything.

And that's how I got roped into helping with the yearbook and how I started getting to know the elite crowd. Of course, I was still the outsider. No one was as aware of that as I was. But it was kind of fun getting some inside glimpses. And Sierra fascinated me the most. I learned quickly that she had a shoe fetish. She was always evaluating everyone's footwear. Including mine.

"Oh, Kenzie," she said to me early on, "don't you know that Birkenstocks are so *yesterday?*"

"Huh?" I looked up from the yearbook page I was rearranging.

"Those sandals." She frowned and shook her head. "All wrong."

"They're comfortable," I said, but what I was really thinking was, *How can anyone actually care about that stuff?*

Sierra laughed. "What does *that* have to do with anything?"

I shrugged and turned my attention back to the layout. But I never wore those Birkenstocks again. But Sierra wasn't always like that. Most of the time she was really sweet. She seemed to appreciate what I was doing for the yearbook. She even brought me Starbucks sometimes. I think she was just concerned over my fashion sense—or lack of it. And when she gave me compliments, she seemed sincere.

"You have the prettiest eyes," she said once when we were working on a particularly tough layout. "The color reminds me of chocolate and caramel." She laughed suddenly. "And now I'm totally craving some Rolos."

The next day she gave me a pack of Rolos, along with my Starbucks.

"Thanks," I told her. "What's this for?"

"To go with your eyes," she said.

And so it went the spring of my junior year. I spent what time I could spare on the yearbook, which was only about an hour every afternoon since I still worked part-time at Little Lambs then. While I really did some serious work on the yearbook, I also spent a whole lot of my time just observing Sierra and her crowd. It didn't bother me that Sierra sometimes brought Ryun along to help. And even though I knew those two were an official couple now, although everyone seemed to think they were as opposite as night and day, I'd still find myself sneaking glimpses of the guy I had obsessed over for so long. And I still wished he could be mine.

I guess that's when Anna and I began drifting apart. She couldn't figure out why I wanted to spend so much time with people who didn't usually give us the time of day. But I couldn't help myself. Something about Sierra's group drew me in. Well, at least as "in" as I could get.

"Just be careful," Anna said quietly as she drove me to the church one day after school. As usual she had stayed later at school, saying she was doing homework in the library, while she waited for me to finish up working on the yearbook.

"What do you mean?" I said, already on edge since she'd been dropping lots of hints about my "new acquaintances." I was starting to wonder if she was jealous. I mean, Sierra hadn't invited *her* to be on the yearbook committee.

Anna stopped her car in front of the big brick church. "I just mean be careful, Kenzie. Things can change pretty quickly in that crowd."

"In that crowd?" I echoed back. "What do you mean?"

"I mean they may not really care about you."

"What if they're not as bad as we thought?" I asked. "What if they're just the same as us, but we've been judging them all wrong?" I couldn't believe I was defending Sierra's group. But Anna was driving me crazy with all her warnings.

That's when I decided to play the Christian card on her. After all, our church was a big part of

her life, and she was always talking about it. And lately she'd been getting really involved with youth group too.

"I mean think about it," I reminded her. "Didn't Jesus say we're supposed to love *everyone?*"

Anna sighed. "Okay, so maybe you're right . . . just be careful, okay?"

"Thanks for the warning," I told her. And then I added, "You know, the weather's been so nice that I'll probably just ride my bike tomorrow."

She nodded, but I could tell I'd hurt her feelings. Maybe she thought refusing a ride was like saying I didn't want to be her friend anymore. It wasn't that I didn't like her. It was just that she seemed so down on me for getting involved in Sierra's group. But I was tired of being on the fringes. A girl had to break out sometime, right? And I'm not talking about zits. Anyway, I waved good-bye to Anna the same as usual that day, but as I walked toward the day-care center, I felt like I was walking away from my old best friend for good.

"Kenny!" yelled Blain from inside the fenced play yard.

I smiled. "Kenny" was my nickname at Little Lambs since some of the kids had a hard time saying "McKenzie" or even "Kenzie." And I didn't mind. It was a whole lot better than "Mac"—a name kids used to try to call me in grade school. A name I hate to this very day.

Within seconds the other Little Lambs kids raced over and started to chant, "Kenny's here! Kenny's here!"

I opened the gate and let myself in, giving hugs to Blain and Sophie and Casey, then all the others who demanded their turns. Since Little Lambs was a day-care center for low-income families in the neighborhood, some of the kids were pretty needy. Sometimes it seemed there were never enough toothbrushes, hugs, or attention to go around. It's like the kids were these little "SpongeBobs" (only they were SpongeBlain and SpongeSophie and SpongeCasey). They soaked up every ounce of love that you could pour out on them.

"It's what Jesus would do," my mom had told the church committee about seven years ago when she'd first proposed the idea. And fortunately, for the dozens of kids who'd benefited over the years, the committee had caught her vision. It hadn't taken long for Little Lambs to open, and my mom had been managing it ever since. My younger sister, Lark, and I had logged in lots of hours here, and my two younger brothers, Aaron and Joshua, nine-year-old twins, still came after school every day.

Josh had recently been telling everyone, "We're too old for this," so Mom decided to give them jobs as "official helpers."

"It might help you earn some Scout badges," she'd suggested. And that was all it took to get those two back on track again.

"Thank goodness you're here, Kenzie," said Mary, a full-time worker. "Linda had to go home early. She has some kind of stomach flu, and your mom's got her hands full with Derrick."

I grinned. Derrick was our current "discipline problem." No one knew what to do with him—well, besides giving him a lot of hugs. What he probably needed was a good spanking, but no one ever got spanked at Little Lambs. It was totally against the rules. But we did use "time-outs" and remove privileges. But the problem was, Derrick refused to stay on the time-out bench.

"Should I go offer to relieve her?" I asked Mary.

"It's up to you," said Mary. "But the kids out here will probably be disappointed if you don't play with them."

And so Mary went to check on my mom while I stayed out and played with the kids. I'd never admit it to anyone now, but it was what I loved the most. Just acting goofy and silly, like I was still a kid myself. I didn't have to worry about hurting Anna's feelings or trying to fit in to Sierra's crowd.

But as I stood out by the fence, holding one end of the jump rope, I noticed a familiar vehicle driving slowly by the church. As if I had antennas, I turned and looked. There, in his dark blue Explorer, was Ryun Lee. And from what I could see through his window, he was smoking a cigarette! Now it wasn't like I never saw kids smoking at and around my school—and not just cigarettes either. But I never would've guessed that Ryun, of all people, would be a smoker. Mostly because he was such a great athlete and pretty serious about it too.

But I suspected that this guy was full of surprises. Maybe that was why he intrigued me so much. It didn't even bother me that he was smoking. There was something invincible about Ryun Lee. Like nothing could touch him or hurt him. Maybe that was just another reason he was so fascinating.

3

My unspectacular junior year was drawing to an end. Not that I cared so much. If anything, I think I just wanted it to be over. I was ready to move on to the college thing. I guess I was relieved when we finished up the yearbook. But there was a bit of sadness too. Even though I'd been pressured to work on it and I wasn't exactly one of the original group, I had taken my contribution fairly seriously and really tried to give it my best effort.

On our last day of "putting the yearbook to bed," as Sierra called it, she was so happy that she wanted everyone to go out to celebrate. But as it turned out, Ryun had to head out of town for a soccer match, Holly and Carin had a cheerleader thing to attend, and everyone else had something going too. I listened as Sierra tried to talk them into ditching their plans and coming with her, but no one seemed willing.

I really felt bad for her. I wanted to raise my hand, wave it back and forth, and say, "Hey, Sierra, I'm here! I'll come with you."

Then to my total surprise, she turned to me and said, "Looks like it's just you and me, Kenzie." She smiled in a hopeful way. "Unless you're bailing on me too."

"No, I'd like to go," I told her.

So it was decided. Just the two of us would go out for dinner that night. I was eager to go but was nervous about making a complete fool of myself. I tried to make small talk and act cool as we walked out to the parking lot—like stuff like this happens to me every day. *Not!* It was the first time I'd ever been inside her beautiful car, although I'd seen it enough times. And it was hard to miss. Everyone knew which car belonged to Sierra since it was a beautifully restored Bentley. A *Bentley*, for Pete's sake! I mean, you could probably add up every single vehicle my parents have ever owned in their entire lives and they wouldn't equal the cost of Sierra's car. And Sierra was only 17!

Well, I'm sure I was grinning like a Cheshire cat as we drove across town. I wanted to roll down the window and wave at everyone, like I was home-coming queen or visiting royalty, but I managed to control myself. Still, I think I might've gasped when she pulled up in front of The Lantern, High-view's most expensive restaurant in town, and handed her keys to a parking valet.

"My treat," she said casually as she adjusted the strap of her purse on her shoulder.

"But I, uh, I—"

"Don't worry," she assured me, looking down at my clothes.

Thankfully I was wearing one of my better outfits, although I was sure Sierra wouldn't consider it fashionable. "You look just fine."

But that wasn't what was bothering me. "But it's so expensive," I said as we walked toward the front door. "And I—"

She turned and smiled at me. "Hey, don't worry. You've been a fantastic help on the yearbook. This is just my way of thanking you."

A man in a dark suit led us to a table covered in white linen and lots of dishes and silverware. I was afraid I was going to trip and fall on my face. But after I actually ate my dinner without spilling my soup or using the wrong fork (I followed Sierra's lead), I finally began to relax.

"It's too bad everybody else didn't come," I told her when our desserts came—mine was something chocolate and decadent. "They're really missing out."

"That's okay," said Sierra. "It's given me a chance to get to know you better."

I nodded, then took a cautious bite, slightly worried that I might pass out from a chocolate overdose. But it was delicious.

"You're really fun to talk with," said Sierra. "Some of my friends aren't very good listeners." Then she laughed. "The truth is, I don't have many close friends."

"What do you mean?" I asked, shocked. "You have tons of friends."

She nodded. "Yeah, I have a lot of friends, but most of them aren't very close."

"Well, maybe that's okay," I told her. "It would be kind of hard to have a lot of close friends, wouldn't it?"

"I guess." But she looked sad.

"I mean, you only have so much time and energy, and if everyone wanted to be your best friend . . . well, it'd probably be exhausting."

"But everyone needs a good best friend," she said in an absent sort of way.

And that's when I began to wonder . . . *who* was her best friend? I knew that lots of girls were always hovering around her, but which of them was her best friend?

"Of course, there's Ryun . . ." Now she smiled. "I couldn't ask for a better friend than him. I don't know why it took me so long to figure it out." She shook her head.

"Figure what out?"

"That Ryun Lee is so totally awesome. I mean, he's kind of quiet, you know, and it takes time to get to know him. But once you do . . ." She sighed. "Well, you wonder why it took you so long."

"Probably because he didn't quite fit in with your other friends?" I offered.

She nodded. "I know what you mean and you're totally right, Kenzie. And it just makes me realize how shallow I've been the past few years. I really don't want to keep being like that. I want to start getting to know people for who they really are, not who we make them out to be."

I wondered if she meant me too, but I didn't ask. That would've been pretty lame. Instead I gave her a bite of my dessert, and we continued to talk.

"I want to make my senior year something really special," she continued. "Something I can take with me always—like the way I take my photographs— something to look back on and remember the good times. Think about it, Kenzie—our junior year is almost done. After this we'll be seniors and then high school will be over and done." She shook her head sadly. "I can hardly bear to think about it. It's been so much fun. Sometimes I wish it would go on forever."

I couldn't really agree with her on that. As far as memories went, I wasn't sure if there was any- thing I particularly wanted to remember about my high school years. At least so far. But I had some hope that things would get better since my life had already perked up a little. After all, here I was having dinner at The Lantern with the most popular girl in school. That was no small accomplishment.

■   ■   ■

In the next couple of weeks as school was winding down, I continued to chat with Sierra every once in a while. Okay, so I wasn't *really* in with her crowd, but sometimes she included me, and she was never rude to me. But to be perfectly honest, most of the time I don't think she even really saw me. It was like I was invisible or something. But sometimes I would just watch her. Not so much when she was with Ryun, because that was too painful. When I studied her in the halls and with her friends, I began to notice that she really didn't seem to have a *best* friend.

In fact, it sometimes seemed like Sierra's friends weren't as devoted as I'd always imagined them to be. And sometimes she seemed unhappy when she was with them. There were even a couple of times when I wondered if her "friends" weren't being kinda rude to her.

I didn't get it. Who wouldn't want to be nice to Sierra Reynolds? But I started to wonder if her old friends might not have grown slightly bored with her over the years. Not that she was boring exactly. But I guess she was a bit shallow. After all, how long could you talk about clothes and shoes and "making memories," anyway?

Still, I was willing to give it my best shot. I would've stepped up to the plate and volunteered to be her new best friend if given the chance. Maybe it was because she was so totally different than me or because her world was so far removed from mine. Things like Bentleys and The Lantern and designer shoes . . . well, those things did intrigue me, just a bit.

Maybe, if I were perfectly honest, I would've admitted that I was even more shallow than Sierra.

4

When I was a little girl and Lark was just a baby, my dad started calling me Mouse. McKenzie Mouse. And I liked it. I'd tiptoe around the house, trying not to wake the new baby, and my dad would say, "Here comes McKenzie Mouse." I'd quietly giggle and continue with our little game. But as I got older, I didn't want to be called Mouse anymore.

I think it started when I heard my Aunt Tina saying that Mrs. Hawkins had mousy brown hair. I knew Mrs. Hawkins, because she was our church secretary, and a lot of people didn't like her. But I wasn't sure what mousy brown hair was. So the next time I saw Mrs. Hawkins, I studied her hair more closely. To my horror I realized it was almost exactly the same color as mine! That meant *I* had mousy brown hair too.

It didn't help that I was painfully shy then. I never wanted to be noticed in school. And if I was called on in class, my face would turn a bright beet red and, with eyes straight forward, I would stutter out the answer. The answer was almost always correct, but I hated being the center of attention. I couldn't understand how other girls seemed to love the limelight. As much as they'd go out of their way to be noticed, I'd go out of my way to blend with the walls.

It got a little better in high school. Not that I gave up being a wallflower completely, but I did begin to relax a little. And by the time I became a junior I tried to convince myself that I really didn't care what people thought. My plan must've been working too, because I think I convinced others, like the yearbook committee, that I was perfectly fine with myself.

"You seem so together," Holly told me one afternoon as we were putting the finishing touches on the layout. School would be out in a few weeks, and we were really pushing to get this yearbook off to the printers.

"Huh?" I asked as I played with the angle of the student council photo.

"I mean, you seem okay with being yourself."

I laughed. "What makes you think that?"

She lowered her voice. "Well, you know how some kids are so into looking perfect, like even their shoes have to be just right."

I glanced over at Sierra, who was in the front of the room, joking around with Ryun. As usual, her shoes were perfect. And expensive too. I turned my attention back to the current page. "And your point is?"

"Well, you don't seem so obsessed with all that."

I shrugged. "Why should I be?"

Actually, I was thinking, *Why bother? There isn't much I can do about it one way or another.* But, hey, if Holly wanted to think I was simply being laid-back, well, fine.

"I just think it's kind of cool."

I looked up and smiled at her. "Thanks."

"Hey, did you hear that Pastor Ken is looking for camp workers for junior high camp?" she asked.

I made a face. "You'd really want to work at junior high camp?"

She lifted her brows mysteriously. "Well, I happened to meet the coolest guy there last year. He was from Oakcrest and a freshman in college. Oh, man, was he ever a hottie. He supervised the sports shop, and I was the lifeguard at the pool. When our shift was over, we'd get together with a bunch of the other workers, mostly high school and college age, and we had some pretty good times."

"Really?"

"Yeah, and you even get paid for working there."

"Seriously, you get paid?"

She nodded. "I heard Pastor Ken saying they still had a few positions open."

I frowned. "But what could I do?"

"You could teach arts and crafts."

I considered this. "Yeah, I suppose I could."

And the next thing I knew I was signed up to

work at Camp Callahan for three weeks during July. Naturally my parents were glad to see me taking an interest in helping out with the junior camp, and my mom even gave me time off from Little Lambs.

"You deserve a break, McKenzie," she assured me. "You've worked at Little Lambs every summer since you were 13. And you're always helping out with the boys and your sister at home."

"I suppose that means it's *my* turn to work at Little Lambs now," said Lark in a sarcastic tone. She didn't look up as she carefully painted a fingernail. The polish was black today. It fit her current mood.

"That's not such a bad idea," said my mom.

"But what if *I* want to go to camp?" demanded Lark, shoving the brush back into the bottle and staring at my mom in a challenging way.

I saw my mom's eyes light up, but she managed to keep her enthusiasm under control. "I suppose that could be worked out."

And so it was arranged that Lark would come for a one-week session while I was working at camp. This seemed quite an accomplishment since my little sister had been getting more and more rebellious since she'd started middle school last fall.

I'd been surprised when my mom said I deserved a break. I'm pretty sure my parents appreciated what I did at home and at Little Lambs, but no one thanked me personally. I'd always thought my contribution to the family was kinda taken for granted. Even before I'd worked at Little Lambs, I'd babysat

Lark and the twins. I'd been doing laundry since I was 11, and I cooked dinner at least once a week. I ran errands and cleaned house.

Not that I was complaining. In some ways it paid off for me. Not just financially, although I'd managed to save quite a bit of money over the years, but also in the area of trust. I was sure my parents would let me do just about anything I asked since they both assumed I was a mature and responsible 17-year-old. And why shouldn't they?

The week before camp Holly called up and asked if I wanted to go shopping for camp clothes.

"Why?" I asked her as I put the twins' Little League uniforms into the washing machine. "I've got plenty of shorts and T-shirts already."

"Well . . ." She paused. "I suppose that's okay if you're not going fishing."

"Fishing?" I slammed down the lid and turned on the washer. "I didn't know we were supposed to go fishing."

"For guys, I mean." Holly laughed. "I just thought you might want something cool to wear, Kenzie. I guess I forgot you're not into that sort—"

"Wait," I said suddenly. I was feeling just a little fed up at the moment. I'd already done three loads of laundry, taken the twins to a Scout thing at the park, dropped Lark off at a friend's, and I still had to be at Little Lambs by 10:30 in order to cook lunch since the regular cook was out with the flu. "I don't get off work until six," I told Holly.

"That's perfect," she said. "I planned to just hang by the pool and work on my tan anyway." She laughed. "Can't go off to Camp Callahan looking like a ghost."

I poked at my pale arm and sighed. "No, I guess not."

"How about if I pick you up at 6:30?" she asked. "We could grab a bite, then hit the mall."

"Sounds good."

I think it was while I was stirring a glucky conglomeration of cheese and milk and butter that I started imagining what it would be like to be someone like Holly or Sierra. A lot of them never had to work summer or part-time jobs. Most of them had their own cars, and many of them had pools. And I suspected *all* of them were having a better summer than me. My idea of a summer *vacation* would be working at the middle-school church camp. But Holly had already told me that was her idea of a summer *job*. Her parents were planning a two-week vacation up in British Columbia during August. Even Anna was going on a big trip to China.

I poured the gloppy mixture over the mountain of macaroni that I'd already boiled and drained and continued to stir. The kitchen was hot and humid and smelled like a dairy farm. I could feel the sweat on my forehead and dripping down my back. I hoped I'd have time to shower before Holly came by. I couldn't bear the idea of going to the mall, smelling like a cow.

"My life totally sucks," I said out loud as I furiously stirred the macaroni and cheese.

That's when I decided it was time for a change.

I mean, you're only a teenager once, right? And I was about to enter my senior year in a school where only a handful of people knew me by name, and those who did probably thought I was a total loser anyway. Okay, maybe a nice, smart, artistic loser who would roll up her sleeves and work hard when they needed something done. But I was sure they thought I would never in a million years be in *their* league. *Still,* I thought as I gave the pot of glop one last stir, *what if I tried?*

At the end of the day I told Mom I had to go home early. "I'm going with Holly to get some things for camp. She's picking me up at 6:30."

My mom frowned, then agreed. "I suppose Mary could drive tonight."

One of my responsibilities at Little Lambs was to transport some of the kids at the end of the day. Some of the parents had jobs that overlapped and they'd arrange for someone to watch their kids until their shifts ended, but a few of the kids had to be dropped off. I never minded this part of the job since I really liked to drive. We'd pile into my mom's old blue van, and I'd put on a Sesame Street CD. Then the kids and I would sing along until I got the last of them home. But I was relieved to have Mary do that for me for once.

I zipped home in time to take a shower and put on my best-looking outfit. Okay, I realized that my flared jeans weren't the hottest label and my T-shirt was most likely uncool, and I'm sure my plain rubber flip-flops would've gotten a thumbs-down from someone like Sierra, but, hey, it was the best I could do. I pulled my still-damp hair back into a ponytail and even put on some lip gloss.

"Big date tonight?" asked Lark as she peered into our bathroom. As usual, I could hear the 13-year-old sarcasm dripping from her.

"No," I told her. "Just going to the mall with a friend."

"Oh."

I could tell she wanted to be invited. I used to invite her to come with Anna and me sometimes, and it had been kind of fun playing big sister, but tonight I wasn't in the mood. "I've got to get some clothes for camp," I told her, as if that explained everything.

"Must be nice," she said as she rolled her eyes.

"Huh?"

"Having money to buy new clothes."

"Look, Lark," I told her impatiently, "you'd have money too if you didn't always blow it on stupid stuff."

"Stupid stuff?" She stepped into the bathroom and glared at me. "Like what?"

I eyed the T-shirt she was wearing. "Like that ridiculous shirt with the shredded sleeves."

"This shirt is *not* ridiculous." She stuck her lip out now.

"Well, I'm sure you paid way too much for it, Lark. Good grief, why didn't you just get one of your old shirts and take the scissors to it?"

She frowned now and actually looked close to tears, but instead she narrowed her eyes. "That just shows how ignorant you are when it comes to fashion, Kenzie." Now she got snooty. "I mean, look at you. I'd be embarrassed to go to the mall looking like *that.*" She shook her head scornfully. "Man, I feel sorry for your friend."

"Whatever." I gave her a shove and slammed the bathroom door in her face.

"Moron!" she yelled.

"Infant!" I yelled back at her. Then I heard a horn honking down below and peered out the window. Holly's red Jeep Wrangler was parked out front with the top down. I burst out the door and past my still-angry little sister, grabbed my purse, and raced down the stairs.

"Loser!" she yelled after me.

It wasn't the best ego-booster to have your little sister giving you a fashion critique and then yelling "Loser!" as you left the house. And it didn't help to see Holly looking cuter than ever in her halter top, with a perfect tan beneath.

"You look great," I told her as I hopped into the Jeep.

She glanced at me and grinned. "You look like you could use some sun." Then she gunned the engine, making my head jerk back as she took off.

That's when I wondered if Holly just wanted me around to make her look better. You know, drag out the plain Jane and suddenly you look like a goddess. Well, whatever.

After getting a bite to eat, Holly was ready to "shop till we flop." And, feeling like her shadow, I began to get seriously depressed as we walked through the mall toward her favorite stores. I

wondered what I was even doing here and who
I was trying to fool.

Finally Holly demanded to know what was wrong.
"You're acting really weird, Kenzie. What's up?"

"I don't know . . ." I pretended to be intensely
interested in a rack of tank tops.

"Come on, Kenzie, what gives? Did I say something to hurt your feelings? I know I can really put
my foot in my mouth sometimes."

"Nooo . . ." I shook my head and looked at her.
"It's just that I feel kinda bummed."

"Bummed?" Her brow seemed to crease with real
concern. "Why?"

"I guess I just feel like such a frump muffin."

She laughed. "A frump muffin? Now that's a
good one." Then she stepped back a bit and studied
me more closely. I felt like a bug under her micro-
scope. "Well . . . ," she began, "there is room for
improvement."

I shrugged. "Hopeless, huh?"

She smiled. "Where there is life, there is hope.
At least that's what my dad says."

"Isn't he a plastic surgeon?"

"Yeah, whatever." She reached over and pulled
out the band that was holding my hair back in a
ponytail.

"Hey." I glanced around, embarrassed that my
still slightly damp and stringy hair was hanging all
over the place.

"You've got nice thick hair, Kenzie. But the color
is . . . well, I won't hurt your feelings, will I?"

"Mousy?" I offered.

Her brows lifted. "I wasn't going to go that far. But let me say it's all wrong."

I nodded. "Yeah, I agree with you."

She brightened. "You do?"

"Yeah. I was blonde when I was little, so I always think of myself like that, but now my hair's pretty dull and boring."

"Hey, I wonder if Charmaine is around." Holly reached in her bag for her cell phone now. Naturally it was a jewel-tone purple—to go with her cheer-leader outfit.

After a brief conversation Holly hung up and turned to me with a big grin. "She was there and she had a cancellation for tomorrow morning at eight. You don't mind getting up that early, do you?"

"For what?"

"To get your hair highlighted."

I considered this.

"I told her exactly what to do," continued Holly. "It's all set . . . unless you're not ready for this yet."

"No, I'm ready," I said quickly.

She patted me on the back. "Good. Now let's do some serious shopping."

"That's another thing." I didn't know how to say this. "But I'm not really much into fashion. . . ."

"Tell me something I *don't* know, Kenzie." She laughed loudly enough to get the attention of the salesclerk. "Just trust me, okay? I might not be as good at this as Sierra, especially when it comes to shoes, but believe me, I know my way around these shops."

And she did. By the time we quit, a few minutes

before closing, I had gone to the ATM machine *three* times! I was loaded down with half a dozen bags from as many different stores. We'd done Gap and American Eagle and Banana Republic and Express and a bunch of others. Holly really seemed to know which store had the best of, well, whatever. For instance, she thought that Banana Republic had the coolest flip-flops this year. We both got a pair—different colors, of course.

"It's not cool to have the exact same ones," she told me when I almost made the fatal mistake of choosing ones like hers.

By the time we piled back into her Jeep we had shorts and jeans and halters and sweatshirts and tennis shoes and flip-flops. And I had actually had fun. It felt like Christmas. I was amazed at how the right items and correct sizes of the right kinds of clothes really did look good on me.

"Man, Kenzie," Holly had said at one point. "You've got a great bod."

Feeling self-conscious, I probably began to slump.

"No, stand up straight," she commanded. "Strut your stuff, woman."

I laughed.

"Really, you are one hot babe. It's just that no one would've ever noticed beneath all those ratty clothes you usually wear." She kind of grimaced then. "Sorry, didn't mean to hurt your feelings."

I shook my head. "No, Holly. You're totally right. I just never knew how to do it any differently." I wanted to hug her but controlled myself.

"Well, you do now, girl!" She stepped back and

peered at me again. "But there's only a week before camp, and we need to get you into the sun."

I looked at my pale midriff, exposed by the cropped shirt I was trying on. A shirt that I knew my parents wouldn't approve of, but what they didn't know wouldn't hurt them either. Besides, I was 17, about to be a senior. It was time for me to make my own decisions. "My mom thinks that suntanning causes cancer," I said, instantly wishing I hadn't. "But I'd work on a tan if I had time. The problem is that I work at the day-care center during the day."

"Ever heard of a tanning booth?" she asked with a twinkle in her eye.

"Really? Do you go to one?"

"Of course. I like to get the real rays when I can, but the rest of the time I rely on SunChasers."

"I've seen their place," I said. "I guess I could try it."

She nodded. "Maybe after you get your hair done tomorrow. They're usually not that busy in the morning. And you could probably get in at least three sessions before we leave for camp."

"Cool."

"Hey," said Holly, "what do you have in the way of bikinis?"

I made a face. "I, uh, well, nothing really."

"You stay right here," she commanded. "I saw a great-looking rack of them out there. I'll be right back."

Bikini? I thought as I waited for her in the dressing room. My dad would probably have a heart attack and keel over. But then, I reminded myself again, what my parents didn't know wouldn't hurt them.

5

"It's perfect!" I told Charmaine after she finished drying my newly highlighted hair. I couldn't believe it was really my hair! It was way better than I'd hoped for. And even though I'd had some second thoughts as I watched myself turn into what looked like some kind of UFO or shortwave transmitter with layers of tinfoil covering my head, it was totally worth it in the end. I absolutely loved it.

"It's gorgeous," she told me as she fluffed the highlights to show off layer after layer of honey gold color. "You have the perfect kind of hair for this. Just remember to use that conditioner I gave you, especially if you go swimming. Chlorine can really mess you up."

I started to get out of the chair.

"Just a minute," she said.

"Huh?"

"You didn't think we were done yet, did you?"

"I, uh, I don't know."

She smiled and pointed to my eyebrows, which I must admit were fairly thick and bushy. I take after my dad. "Don't you want to do something about those?"

I shrugged. "I'm not sure. What did you have in mind?"

"A little wax."

"Wax?" All I could think of was the stuff my mom used to put on our hardwood floors before she discovered a handier product.

She nodded. "We'll wax them to get rid of some of those unwanted hairs, and then maybe tweeze just a little if needed."

"Uh . . . okay."

The waxing and tweezing ended up being a lot more painful than I'd expected, but when she was done, it was worth the pain. "Wow," I said as I looked in the mirror. "That's way better."

"Okay, one more thing," Charmaine said.

"Really?"

"Well, Holly told me to give you the works."

"What now?"

Then she led me over to a whole line of beauty products and cosmetics. "You don't really need much, McKenzie, but we should get you started on some basics."

By the time I left her salon, I not only had great hair and more delicate eyebrows, but a skin-care regime and some very expensive blush, lip gloss, concealer, mascara, and eye makeup.

"Just the basics," she had said again as she handed me the small bag. And, as instructed by Holly the previous day, I gave her a generous tip. Then, feeling a lot poorer but much more glamorous, I headed over to the tanning salon where I lied, as instructed by Holly, and told them I was 18 and plunked down even more money for a package of tanning sessions and some very expensive super-speed tanning lotion.

It was kind of scary getting into that strange contraption for the first time. It reminded me of a piece of hospital equipment. But then this was a time for firsts, and I still remembered Holly's challenge last night—"unless you're not ready for this yet." Well, determined to show her and myself and the whole world that I *was* ready, I put on my protective goggles and turned on the machine. As the lights and the heat came on and the fans hummed loudly, I hoped I wasn't doing any permanent skin damage. Even more, I hoped my parents wouldn't get too upset at me.

■ ■ ■

My parents weren't angry. Maybe a little surprised. I didn't tell them about the tanning thing, but there was no way to hide my hair. But they both seemed to think it was okay.

"It's nice to see you caring about your appearance," said my dad. "God made you a pretty girl, and there's nothing wrong with enjoying it."

My mom nodded but was a little less convinced.

"I'm still getting used to your hair, honey. But it's pretty. It reminds me of when you were little."

"What'd you do to your hair?" demanded Josh when he came downstairs and threw his baseball mitt onto the counter. I suspected by the uniform that this was game day.

"Lightened it," I told him, giving it a toss over my shoulder and still enjoying how good it felt.

"Where's Kenzie?" teased Aaron when he saw me. "What have you done with my big sister?"

"She was abducted by aliens," I told him with a scowl. "And they sent me back in her place because *I love to eat nine-year-old boys for lunch.*"

"Oooh, I'm scared," said Aaron.

"How do you feel about driving nine-year-old boys to their Little League game?" asked my mom.

"Oh, Mom," I began to protest.

"I'm only asking you to drop them off," she said quickly. "Your dad has to meet with an electrical sub this morning and I have garden club, but one of us will pick them up."

"Can I get a ride too—?" Lark stopped when she came into the kitchen. "Man, Kenzie, what have you done to your hair?"

I could tell by the tone of her voice that she wasn't being critical for once. I turned around to face her now. "I got it highlighted."

Her eyes widened as she came closer. "Wow, you look really different."

I shrugged. "Yeah, well, change is good, right?"

She nodded. "I like it." Then she turned to our

mom. "I want to do that too. Can I get my hair high-lighted like Kenzie's?"

I just shook my head and grabbed an apple out of the fridge as my mom began reminding Lark for the hundredth time that I was going to be a senior, whereas Lark was still in middle school.

"I get sick and tired of being treated like a baby!" she yelled as she stomped from the room.

Josh and Aaron were snarfing down peanut-butter-and-jelly sandwiches that my mom had whipped out in 30 seconds. "Drink your milk," Mom reminded them as she filled their thermoses with Kool-Aid and ice.

"You guys ready to go yet?" I asked, impatient to get my chauffeuring over with.

"Yeah!" Josh grabbed up his mitt. "The coach'll make us sit on the bench if we're late for batting practice."

"When have you ever been late for batting practice?" asked my mom as she put the milk jug back in the fridge and handed Aaron the thermos.

"Never," said Aaron. "But let's keep it that way."

"I'm coming," yelled Lark as we were going out the door. "Not that anyone cares about me."

"Lark gets the front seat," I warned my brothers as we hurried out to the van.

"Thanks," said Lark as she slid in. "I really do like your hair."

"Well, give it some time," I told her. "Maybe Mom will soften up after she gets over the shock of seeing me."

Lark rolled her eyes. "Yeah, like maybe when I'm 16."

"That's not so far off," I warned her.

"Puleeze." She leaned back into the seat. "I wish I was 16. I think I'd get a car and just drive away somewhere."

I laughed. "Well, you better get a job before you get a car."

"You should talk. You don't even have a car, Kenzie."

"That's because I've been putting my money into savings."

"How much did it all cost?" she asked in a quiet voice.

"What?" I turned and looked at her. "What do you mean?"

"I saw all those bags and that cool stuff. And I could tell it wasn't cheap. Come on, Kenzie, tell me how much you put out for everything."

"I—uh—I'm not sure," I told her. And that was true. I was almost afraid to add it all up. I knew how much I'd taken from the ATM and I still had some money left. But it made me feel slightly ill to think of how much I'd spent.

"Hey, don't feel bad," she said suddenly. "Man, Kenzie, you never buy anything. I think it's cool that you splurged. And you look really good too. I'd have done the same thing if I was you, only I'd have done it a lot sooner!"

Some consolation coming from a 13-year-old. Especially one with a chip on her shoulder.

I dropped the brothers off, then turned back to Lark. "So, where are you going?"

"Do you think you could pick up Lacy?"

I frowned. "I thought Mom and Dad didn't want you hanging with her."

Lark groaned. "They just don't understand. Lacy is perfectly fine. She gets good grades and everything."

"Uh-huh?" Still, I wasn't convinced. Last I'd heard Lacy and Lark had gotten in trouble for skipping school one afternoon toward the end of the school year.

"Please, Kenzie." She put on her pitiful face now.

I shook my head.

"Crud, and I was just starting to think you were cool."

I laughed. "Cool has nothing to do with it."

"Look, Kenzie, it was *my* idea to skip that day. And Lacy really got in trouble for it too."

"Really?"

"Honest. We just want to go to the mall and maybe go to a movie. It's not like we're going to go rob a bank or something."

I considered this. "Okay, I'll take you guys there, but you've got to promise not to do anything I wouldn't do."

"You mean like get my hair bleached?"

"Well, don't do that."

"Yeah, yeah. We'll be perfect little angels, Kenzie. I promise."

And so, knowing full well that my parents would not approve, I picked up Lacy, who really did seem to be behaving like a perfect angel, and dropped both of them off at the mall.

"Thanks, Kenzie," said Lark with a smile. "Hey, do you think I could borrow 10 bucks?"

I frowned at her.

"Just until I get paid from Little Lambs." Lacy was waiting and Lark's eyes were pleading.

"Okay," I told her, fishing in my bag for my wallet. "But don't pay me back. It's a gift."

"You're the best sister," she said, then turned to join her friend.

Yeah, I was thinking as I pulled back onto the street with Mom's big old van, *I may be the best sister when I'm giving out rides and money. But just wait until we both want into the bathroom at the same time.*

At the first stoplight I glanced at myself in the rearview mirror again. I hoped this wasn't becoming a habit, but I was just so amazed at how a morning at Charmaine's and the tanning booth had transformed me. Incredible. Of course, the new clothes didn't hurt either. I really looked different!

Then I heard a horn honking from behind. The light was green. I realized I better focus on my driving instead of myself.

Since my mom wouldn't be needing her van for a while, I decided to take the long way home. I guess I was hoping I might see someone I knew, possibly show off my new look. But no one seemed to be noticing, and I suspected that an old blue Ford van wasn't exactly the kind of vehicle that drew much attention. Feeling a bit silly and shallow about becoming so self-absorbed, I decided to turn around and go straight back home. So I turned down a street I'd usually avoid. Kind of a trashy area with cheap bars, gas stations, and diners. I was surprised to see a vehicle that looked just like Ryun's, pulling into a cruddy-looking place called the Crow Bar. I figured no way could that be him. Then I saw the plates, which weren't snob plates but did have three letters I'd trained myself to recognize—QKB, which I like to think of as Quick Kicking Boy. Okay, maybe it was silly, but it worked for me. Then I knew it really was Ryun's car. So I slowed down a bit and watched as, sure enough, Ryun emerged from the Explorer. He waved to a bunch of older guys that I've never seen before. They were all Korean, I was guessing, and they seemed to know Ryun. Then the bunch of them walked right into the bar.

Weird, I was thinking as I continued driving home. What would Ryun be doing with a bunch of old guys and going into a bar? And how was he getting into the bar since he wasn't even close to 21? But then I thought, *Maybe those are some of his relatives, and maybe they're going in there for some sort of family thing. Maybe they make exceptions during the day.* After all, what did I know about bars?

Convinced that Ryun was probably doing something normal, like attending a birthday party or bar mitzvah—okay, so he wasn't Jewish, but I figured he wasn't doing anything illegal. After all, he was Ryun Lee. How could he possibly do anything wrong?

6

The official first day of my newly reinvented life started on the day Holly and I headed off to Camp Callahan. We rode up there in her Jeep. "That way we'll have wheels once we're up there," she had told me earlier.

But I still remember how giddy I felt when I saw her Jeep parked in front of my house with the top down that day. I couldn't believe I was going off for three weeks—*with* my parents' blessing—and all for the purpose of having fun and getting paid too. Life was good!

"You look incredible," said Holly as I threw my gear into the back of her Jeep. She hadn't seen me since I'd gotten my hair highlighted.

"Thanks," I told her as I hopped in. "Thanks to you and Charmaine, I should say."

"Hey, we might've lent a helping hand, but you're the one who had all the right stuff. Who knew what a babe was hiding underneath your old Kenzie uniform?"

She'd already put the top down on her Jeep and I still remember how the two of us threw back our heads and yelled, *"Woo-hoo!"* as she drove out of town.

And so it went for the next three weeks. Some of the counselors constantly complained about the campers, but I was used to working with kids and really thought these were better behaved than most of the kids we take care of at Little Lambs. Plus, they seemed to enjoy the projects I planned for them at the craft shack. To be honest, I was having nearly as much fun with the kids as I was with my older friends when our daily jobs were done. Usually we'd drive up to the lake to cool off and then go to town for pizza or burgers. It felt like a working vacation.

Naturally I hung with Holly during our off time and when guys noticed her, they noticed me too. But having Holly around like that, almost 24-7, was like taking a crash course in how to act cool (when you're really not). And I proved to be a pretty fast learner. By the time my little sister showed up for her camping session, which happened to be my last week, I was definitely part of this crowd. I even had two guys pursuing me—at the same time. What a trip!

"Wow," said Lark when I welcomed her to camp. "You seem so different, Kenzie."

I winked at her. "Maybe I am."

"This is my sister," I heard Lark telling a new friend she'd met on the bus ride up. "Her name's Kenzie, and she teaches arts and crafts here." It was fun hearing the pride in Lark's voice. In some ways, I think that meant as much to me as anything.

"So, come on by the craft shack sometime," I told Lark and her friend, "and we'll make something really cool."

By the time our three weeks ended, I had decided that neither of the guys who'd been trying to gain my attention were really my type. Ross had been fun in a goofy clownish sort of way. And Chris was definitely an ego-booster since he was a college guy. But I wasn't nearly as sad to say good-bye as I put on. I hugged my new friends and told them I'd miss them. Then Holly and I piled our bags into the back of her Jeep and waved farewell.

On our way home Holly and I stopped for lunch in this little town called Greenwood. Across the street from the deli was a tattoo and piercing shop. And just as we were finishing off our lunch, I told her I'd been considering getting my belly button pierced. So she grabbed my arm and tugged me from the table even before I'd even finished my last bite. And then we actually lied about our ages and got our belly buttons pierced together. Of course, I didn't plan on telling anyone. Especially my parents. They were already starting to scratch their heads about me lately, but a pierced belly button . . . well, believe me, that'd be way beyond their comfort level.

After we got home from camp, Holly continued to call me and even included me in with her other friends. I found myself tagging along with her as she spent time with Carin and Alyssa and Sierra. And to my astonishment, they all seemed to accept me! It was like my makeover was my magic ticket into their world. We went shopping together, had lunch, went to parties, and hung out by Holly's pool. I was living the good life and, believe me, I wasn't complaining one little bit. I made sure that these girls never set foot inside my house, never saw my parents, or got even a glimpse of how my family lived. I almost felt as if I was living a double life. But it was so worth it!

I got a little nervous about losing my new position in their group when it was time for Holly to go on vacation with her parents. She'd been the one to really let me into this inner circle of friends, and now I had no one. Or so it seemed. But then Sierra jumped in and took over as soon as Holly was out of the picture.

"I think this is a shopping day," she told me one morning on the phone.

"Really?" I tried not to consider my steadily shrinking bank account.

"Yes. For one thing, they're having a sale at Saks, and for another thing, you really need some new sandals for the party on Friday."

I laughed. "What party?"

"Don't worry," she said quickly. "I'll explain it all after I pick you up."

So we spent a day at the coolest stores. If I thought Holly's taste was expensive, Sierra's was totally uptown and out of my price range. Mostly

I watched her shop and told her she looked fantastic in everything she tried on (without lying too!). But before the day ended, she did talk me into purchasing a few items.

"I want you to come to a party at my house on Friday," she told me. "Actually, it's my parents' party, but I get to invite a few close friends over."

Close friends, I was thinking hopefully. She actually considered me a *close* friend! And so I dressed up in the very outfit that Sierra had picked out for me that day, and feeling a bit like a fish out of water, I had my dad drop me off—not at her door, that would be too embarrassing—down the street a ways. It was a beautiful summer evening. I told myself I was doing this just to enjoy the walk.

I probably needed those extra few minutes to prepare myself for Sierra's house. I could tell by the neighboring homes that it was going to be spectacular. And I wasn't disappointed. But I wouldn't call it a home as much as a mansion. From where I was standing out on the sidewalk, it was huge and impressive. Like everything else in Sierra's life, it seemed totally unlike my own— as if her world were a foreign country I'd like to visit but where I don't even speak the language. Like all the stuff she knows about fashion and designers and style, especially shoes. But I really wanted to know all about those things too. I guess I *was* pretty shallow.

I thought I was going to faint when I stepped into her house. I'd never been inside anything so amazingly grand. With its sweeping staircase and wide-open rooms, it was like something you'd see in a movie. Not only did everything match perfectly, it all looked extremely expensive and somewhat fragile. I broke out in a sweat when I first walked in. I was so worried that I might accidentally bump into what I was sure must be a priceless Asian vase. I could just imagine it shattering with a loud crash onto the marble floor of the foyer. There were antiques everywhere and Oriental carpets and chandeliers and original pieces of art like you'd see in a gallery or museum. I was blown away.

And then I met her parents. Whoa! Now if I had parents like that I never would've hidden out during band concerts or open houses. I would've proudly introduced them to everyone I knew. But Sierra seemed to just take them for granted as she introduced them to me. I'm sure my palms were clammy when I shook their hands. And I'm sure they wondered why Sierra had decided to hang with someone like me. But they were perfectly charming, and by the end of the evening I actually thought they liked me. I know I liked them. Not just their looks, although they both would've been perfectly at home on the slick pages of something like *Vogue,* a magazine I'd never purchased but had noticed a recent issue, along with others, in Sierra's bedroom. Yes, Sierra had her own private bathroom too, complete with sunken tub and steam shower and, let me tell you, that girl had it all!

Of course, after seeing Sierra's impressive parents and home, I knew without a doubt that I would do whatever it took to keep her from meeting my less-than-ordinary parents. *No way* did I want Sierra to darken the door of my house. Not if I could help it.

I mean, everyone's heard of theme parks, right? But I happen to live in a theme house. Every room in my house has a different theme to it. For instance, the first room you see—the living room—has a Victorian theme. Not the kind of Victorian where everything is velvet and tassels and antiques . . . that might actually be interesting. No, my living room is more of an '80s type of Victorian, where everything is slipcovered in fabric that's suffocating in cabbage roses. Plus, little white lacy things called *doilies* are on every possible surface, and on top of those doilies are the *knickknacks*—or at least that's what my mom calls them. I call them dust catchers and just plain ugly. But then I don't spend much time in that room either.

Let me continue. Then we come to the dining and kitchen areas. Now the theme here is apples. Lots and lots of apples. We have apples on the wall-paper and curtains, little red apple knobs on the cabinets, and an apple cookie jar and teakettle, and well, I'm sure you get the picture.

Then there's the downstairs bathroom and laundry area. Welcome to Gooseville, where we have wallpaper borders of geese with pink ribbons around their necks. Plus, there's a life-size stuffed goose I call Henrietta, who sits in the corner of the bathroom. I keep checking, but she hasn't laid an egg yet. And, of course, there's other goose paraphernalia everywhere you look. Honk-honk—puleeze.

But that's not half as bad as the bathroom that

Lark and I share upstairs. It's got, of all things, a teddy-bear theme. Sure we liked it when we were in grade school, but don't even get me going now. Let's just say it would be really embarrassing if one of my new friends ever wanted to use it. Even the twins' bathroom is better with its yellow rubber ducky theme. I'd much prefer that, except that it always smells like dirty socks and musty tennis shoes. And I'm sure it will only get worse over the years.

It's some consolation that my room is themeless. And that's only because I stripped down the pink ballerinas years ago. I'd always thought they were ridiculous anyway, since I've never had the slightest interest in ballet. Soccer would've been more appropriate, but that's what the twins have in their room.

Anyway, I knew it was going to be tricky being friends with someone like Sierra because I'd have to keep my home and family totally out of the picture. But I also knew it was the only way this thing was going to work for me. If I'd thought my parents were a little frumpy before, I knew without a doubt they were totally and irreparably *uncool* now. No way was I going to let Sierra or Holly or Carin see what the Parker homestead looked like. It would ruin everything. I realized then that being friends with Sierra was my ticket out of my boring little world. It was my big chance to have something more. And, believe me, I wasn't going to blow it. At least not on purpose!

degrees of betrayal

Summer progressed, and I slowly became more comfortable in my own skin. I was still leading something of a double life—hanging with the rich and famous while keeping my own middle-class identity undercover. But by the time August rolled around, I thought I had this thing under control. Then I went down to the University of Virginia for visitation weekend—and suddenly things changed. Man, did they change!

Sure, I tried to act natural, but I was in total shock. I'd come down here thinking this college visit would be pretty boring, but then someone (my guardian angel maybe) went and paired me off with none other than the guy of my dreams—Highview High's soccer king *Ryun Lee!*

Talk about unreal! Who would've thought something like this could happen to me? But there I was, staring into the face of the coolest guy on the planet—the guy I'd had a secret crush on for, well, like forever. I casually said, "Hey," as I joined him in the backseat of our escort's car, but I couldn't help thinking, *What is up with this? Have I died and gone to heaven?*

Just the same, I couldn't figure out why Ryun Lee would be wasting his time visiting a college like the University of Virginia when everyone knew he was getting some incredible scholarship offers from the really big schools—like Duke.

I had to remind myself to play it cool. No way was I going to blow the new image I'd worked so hard to create over the last couple of months. You are a new woman, McKenzie Parker, I told myself. And your time has finally come!

"How's your game going this summer?" I asked as our escort, a Billy something or other, put the car into gear.

Ryun gave me a confused look. "It's going fine."

I nodded and leaned back, thankful that I'd decided to wear the sundress Sierra talked me into buying on our most recent shopping spree. It was a two-piece number with a halter top that fit like skin and an adorable little skirt that swirled nicely and showed off my tanned legs. Sierra assured me it was perfect for me and even said the color brought out the gold flecks in my brown eyes. She also insisted on picking out the coolest shoes I'd ever owned in my life—Nine Wests with high heels and skinny straps. Of course, because Sierra helped, they went perfectly with the sundress.

As I sat in the car, I felt like laughing. Ryun looked so dazed and confused, like he couldn't place who I was or how I knew him. It was obvious he had no idea who the strange chick sitting beside him really was. I felt sorry for him, so I finally gave him a break. "You don't remember me, do you?"

He made a funny face. "Well, I'm not sure. You seem familiar."

I stretched out my hand. "McKenzie Parker."

He nodded and shook my hand, holding on a second or two longer than you'd normally do. And the feeling of him holding my hand like that and looking into my eyes made me feel warm and tingly all over. Almost dizzy.

"McKenzie Parker," he repeated, but it was obvious he was still clueless.

"Remember we worked on the yearbook together?"

His raised eyebrow showed he was even more surprised. *THAT McKenzie?* I could tell he was thinking. But since he's a gentleman, he didn't even mention my prior life as the invisible girl.

Still, it was fun watching him study me, as if seeing me for the first time. And I got this feeling that he liked what he saw too. Just the same, I was careful to keep my distance. I mean, as much as I liked Ryun and have always liked Ryun, I didn't want to move in on Sierra's turf. Everyone knew that she and Ryun had been a "thing" since the spring of junior year. And I knew enough about Sierra and her friends to know that it wouldn't be good for me if I did something sleazy like that. But it sure wasn't *my* fault we'd been stuck together for the evening.

Besides, we were only doing a little tour of the campus and then heading over to a party at a frat house. Totally innocent.

After a few minutes, I couldn't help but bring up Sierra's name. For one thing, I was curious. If they were still dating, and I assumed they were since she hadn't told me otherwise, then why didn't he invite her to come along with him? Besides that, I wanted to see how he reacted. Because, although I certainly wasn't an expert on these matters, I thought Ryun Lee was actually *flirting* with me. He'd already complimented me on my new look several times. There was just something about those smoldering dark eyes that told me he liked the new me.

"It's so strange," I said. "Here Sierra and I have been spending all this time together lately, and now to see you . . ."

I saw something flicker in his eyes. Almost like when one of my little brothers gets caught with his hand in the cookie jar. "You *know* Sierra?" he asked. I could tell by the way he said "know" that he wasn't talking about casually knowing Sierra. Everyone in school KNEW Sierra. He meant, *Do you know her, as in are you friends with her?*

So I told him a bit about my summer, how Holly and I became friends and then how I'd spent time with Sierra more recently. "It's not like we're best friends or anything like that," I assured him. "We've just been hanging together more since Holly's gone on vacation."

But what I didn't tell him was that I wouldn't mind being her best friend or that I was curious to know more about her. And who better to ask than her "supposed" boyfriend? "Supposed," since he still hadn't said anything firm about them still being together, which seemed a little weird. Even so, I didn't ask why she wasn't in Virginia for the weekend.

But I did ask Ryun what Sierra Reynolds was really like. Again he seemed surprised, and suddenly I felt a little lame for even asking. Like I was prying into something that was none of my business. So I was relieved when he changed the subject and began asking me about me. Like he actually wanted to know who I was. At first I fended off his questions since I wasn't about to expose myself to this cool guy. "But what are you into, Kenzie?" he persisted. "You know that soccer is the thing I live for, but how about you? What do you really love?"

Besides you? I was thinking. But thankfully I didn't say that.

He reached over and put his hand on my arm. "Really, I want to know."

Finally, I couldn't stand it. I mean, I did want to get to know this guy I'd watched from afar for so long. And, totally forgetting my promise to play it cool, I threw all my cards (well, almost) on the table. I must've told him my whole life story. I even told him about how much I love working with the kids at my mom's day-care center.

"It's called Little Lambs," I explained. "And it's for kids whose parents can't afford day care. The families have to fit a certain economic profile, and then our church subsidizes the difference. But the thing is," I told him with enthusiasm, "it's like one of the best day-care facilities in the entire city. It's even won some awards. And we've had wealthy people beg my mom to let their kids in."

He laughed and his eyes looked warm and happy. "That's so cool, Kenzie."

"And the kids are so great," I continued. "I love working with them. It's like they totally appreciate everything. Sure there are some kids who act up, but some of them have some hard stuff going on in their lives. It's like Little Lambs is their safe haven, you know?"

He nodded. "I'd like to see the place sometime."

I smiled and told him that I'd be happy to give him the complete tour anytime he'd like. Then he told me a lot about himself too. He admitted that, even though he was popular because of his soccer skills, it was hard being Korean in a mostly Caucasian school. He still felt like an outsider a lot of the time.

"No way," I said.

"It's true," he assured me. "I know how to act like I think everything's cool, but underneath there's a different person. I try to make sure that no one knows the real Ryun Lee."

I frowned. "So, tell me, am I talking to the real Ryun Lee right now?"

He grinned. "Maybe."

"Well, just for the record, I like who I see. I don't think there's anything you could tell me that would make me dislike you. I think you're totally cool."
Oh no, I warned myself, *don't go gushing now.*

But Ryun seemed to like my praise.

"And even if you didn't play soccer," I continued, "I'd still think you were totally cool."

"Somehow I can believe that," he told me, "especially coming from you."

■   ■   ■

Before the night was over, I felt like I knew Ryun Lee almost as well as I knew myself. And I could feel myself falling—make that plummeting—in love with the guy I'd had a crush on for ages. The guy I talked to in my dreams and in my head every time he walked by.

We talked for several hours, but it seemed like minutes. I felt like Cinderella, knowing our time would end and we'd both turn back into ourselves and go back home to Highview. Then Sierra, the incredibly cool and popular Sierra, would have her guy back by her side again and I'd just be on the fringes, where I usually was. Still, why not make the best of tonight? I asked myself. Really make it a night to remember?

And so when Ryun offered me some spiked punch, I figured, hey, why not? I mean, here we were at college. The punch must have loosened me up even more. It's like I didn't care if he knew *everything* about me. So I totally spilled my guts to him. I even told him about my boring family and how I'd worked so hard to transform my appearance over the summer. I told him how badly I wanted to escape my boring life and have some fun. And he totally got it. I knew he did because earlier that day he had told me, "You know, Sierra would never get this, but there are just times when you have to go out there on your own. No group. Nobody else. Just you. Figure it out on your own . . ."

"You're right," I had agreed. "Sierra would never get that. She always has to have a group around. I don't think she ever spends any time alone."

So that evening we ditched the frat party. We went to a nearby park and just sat in swings and talked, openly and honestly. Like two real people who happened to like each other. And suddenly I got this urge to fold down the waist of my skirt, just enough to show him the gold ring that goes through my belly button.

When I looked into his eyes, I could tell he was impressed. And then the strangest thing happened. Ryun leaned forward until all I could smell was his musky cologne. Gently taking my chin in his hand, he kissed me. Not just one of those you're-a-nice-little-sister kisses either. A *real* kiss. And I didn't resist. Not in the least.

For a split second after that kiss, I felt a little guilty about Sierra. *But it isn't as if she and Ryun are engaged or anything,* I argued with myself. *And as far as I know this is still a free country.* Romances came and went like the weather—especially at High High. *For all I know, Ryun's already broken up with her,* I told myself, although Sierra hadn't mentioned this, even though I saw her only a few days ago. But then again, she hadn't come with him on this weekend either. Didn't that mean something?

That night I finally fell asleep, dreaming about Ryun Lee, the soccer king and me (the miraculously transformed Kenzie) walking down the halls of High High together. And life was truly beautiful!

I wished I'd thought to ask Ryun how
he was getting home. Maybe I could've caught
a ride with him and avoided this tedious bus ride,
sitting next to a woman who smelled like she hadn't
bathed in weeks. But then again, maybe I needed
the time to think. I had such a mix of feelings. I
really liked the new me, at least mostly, but sometimes I felt worried too. Like what if I was missing
something? And what about Sierra? It was kind of
confusing.

   I wondered if Anna was right. Would I be sorry
later on down the line? I couldn't help but feel guilty
about that kiss either. Okay, guilty as well as good.
I wouldn't undo it for anything. It was like a dream
come true. But on the other hand, I could've made
a really big mistake. For all I knew Sierra and

Ryun were still an item and I might be seen as the cheating friend if word ever got out. Although I sure wasn't planning on telling anyone. It was shocking really, like who was this girl who was suddenly kissing forbidden boys and keeping secrets? Who was I becoming?

Once I got home I tried to put those thoughts behind me as I spent the day unpacking, doing laundry, and daydreaming, but I couldn't stop thinking about Ryun. I imagined us together, showing up on the first day back at school, walking hand in hand into the senior hall as if it were the most normal thing in the world. There was definitely something between us. I knew it! I could feel it deep inside of me. And I knew this was my chance of a lifetime. So why shouldn't I go for it? I felt almost certain that he and Sierra had already broken up. Either shortly before the University of Virginia trip or after he got home. I was positive those two were history. Why else would he have kissed me like that?

The second day after the Virginia visit, Lark yelled, "Phone!" and I desperately hoped it was Ryun. But it was Sierra, and she wanted me to go shopping with her. I didn't know what to say.

"They're having a trunk show of the latest Manola Blahniks and I'm dying to see them up close and personal," she told me with the kind of breathless excitement that only someone like Sierra can get over footwear.

I told Sierra I'd be glad to go with her. If nothing else, I might discover what was happening between her and Ryun.

"Don't expect me to buy any shoes though," I warned her when she picked me up in her Bentley.

"Why not?" she asked as she pulled out into the street.

"I think they're a little out of my price range."

She laughed. "Kenzie, there are only a few things in life that you can't pay too much for. Shoes are one of them."

I gave a half laugh. "What are the others?"

She smiled. "Oh, I don't know. Maybe friends and good times."

I wasn't sure about that. Did she mean you can "buy" friends and good times? I wondered. If so, I sure didn't want to be in that category. Or maybe she meant it in a more metaphorical way. But I didn't have time to think about it any longer because she began asking me about my visit to Virginia.

And as she did, three things became obvious:

1. She and Ryun were still an item.

2. Ryun wasn't taking her along with him on his university visits. That gave me some hope that a breakup might be coming.

3. She had no idea that Ryun and I spent any time together this past weekend. She didn't even know for sure which school Ryun went to. I should have been relieved, but instead I was irritated. Did that mean I was chopped liver? That Ryun wouldn't even think to mention that he saw me at the University of Virginia? But then I realized. So what would he say, anyway? "Oh, by the way, Sierra, I hung out with Kenzie Parker this weekend and we kissed passionately"? Yeah, like that was going to happen.

kenzie's story

For three days after our Virginia visit, I raced to the phone every time it rang, thinking it was going to be Ryun. Lark just rolled her eyes at me, ironic since *she* was the one who usually raced for the phone. But after nearly a week of waiting and hoping that Ryun would call and even being tempted to call him myself, I realized that what happened in Virginia meant nothing to him. The sooner I got over it the better.

Besides, I told myself, *at least I still have Sierra.* And hanging with Sierra was good medicine for getting over Ryun. Believe me, hearing her going on and on about Ryun—how cool he was, what a great soccer player he was, yada-yada—well, it was really rubbing against me. It seemed to be turning what was once tender and sore into a hard callus. It was making me tough. Or so I tried to convince myself.

I also tried to console myself with my new position in the High High scheme of things. At least that still seemed secure. And judging by the way things were going with Sierra, it was obvious she still wanted to be my friend.

And so, I was thankful to have her friendship. In a way, I felt like I'd worked pretty hard just to get it. I'd even skipped out on church a lot lately, and I'd seen Anna only a time or two, and then we didn't say much. It was pretty uncomfortable. I didn't think Anna approved of the new and improved Kenzie, but she didn't say anything mean. She just seemed a little sad, like I didn't have time for her anymore. And I guess she was right. I barely had time to keep up with everything it took just to be a part of Sierra's group.

One day, just a few days before school started, Sierra and I were sitting out by her pool, giving ourselves pedicures. She was talking about how busy the cheerleaders were right now, getting everything together for the pep rally next week.

"Why didn't you ever go out for cheerleading?" I asked as I painted my big toe a bright red called "Bombshell Betty." I felt absolutely certain Sierra would have been picked if she'd tried.

"Cheerleading is so ordinary," she said as she experimented with "Flaming Coral," holding her foot up for my approval.

"Looks good."

"And besides," she continued, "I've got my responsibilities as council president and the yearbook committee and—"

"And besides," interrupted her younger sister, Jacqueline, who had sneaked up behind us, "Sierra's got two left feet."

"Jacqueline! Quit eavesdropping!" Sierra scolded her.

I didn't want to hurt her sister's feelings, but I couldn't help myself and I laughed too. "Really?" I asked Sierra. "Do you really have two left feet?"

"I wouldn't exactly say—"

"I would!" Jacqueline said with a big grin. "She *does* have two left feet, Kenzie. Haven't you ever seen her dance?"

"Get a life, Jacqueline," said Sierra in a bored voice.

So maybe that *was* the real reason Sierra hadn't gone out for cheerleading, because obviously she was popular enough to get elected, if she could do the required routines. But maybe she really would've liked to have been a cheerleader and felt left out. For some reason that seemed like a revelation to me—I mean, it was hard to imagine Sierra ever feeling left out of anything. But then why couldn't she admit this to me? Especially if I really was her best friend? Then I stopped myself. *Maybe she is being honest with me. Maybe she really does prefer student council and the yearbook committee to jumping around in a short skirt.* I had to admit that seemed the most respectable answer to me. And one that matched with who I thought Sierra was. Whatever her reasons, I knew I was lucky to have her as my friend. And it wasn't a thing I took for granted.

But our friendship still felt awkward sometimes. And I still felt guilty over *the kiss* every time I saw her. I tried to forget it and put it behind me, convincing myself that it was just a onetime shot. But even so it haunted me. And I freaked over how I would act around Ryun once school started.

And then suddenly it was the night before the first day of school and I was a mess. I hadn't seen Ryun once since the night of *the kiss*. What if I fell apart when I saw him tomorrow? What if Sierra saw me acting like a complete idiot and figured everything out?

I think I'm going to be sick.

9

The seniors were supposed to dress in togas on the first day of school. Don't ask me why—it was just something that had been going on since the Stone Age. But every year the theme for the togas was slightly different. This year we were supposed to wear prison togas. Like what was that supposed to mean? I felt seriously irritated with this tradition since I was dying to show off one of the new outfits I'd gotten while shopping with Sierra. Unfortunately, that would have to wait.

Anyway, Sierra had insisted that she and I wear matching togas. Her design, of course. So on the first day of my senior year I was wearing a black-and-white-striped toga.

"Cool," said Aaron when I came down for breakfast.

"You look like a zebra," offered Josh.

"You look ridiculous," said Lark.

"Thanks, everyone." I ate one of Mom's home-made granola bars and swigged down some apple juice.

"You're really wearing that thing to school?" asked Lark, looking stunned.

"Everyone is wearing them," I assured her.

"Why?"

"Tradition." Just then I heard Sierra honking for me in the driveway.

"Man, I hope this isn't a setup," said Lark with seriously worried eyes.

"See ya!" I called as I grabbed up my bag and headed out the door.

Thankfully I could see that it wasn't a setup, as Lark had suggested, because Sierra was wearing her matching toga too.

"Hey," I said as I climbed into her car, "we look like twins."

"Actually, they're different," she told me as she pulled out.

"Yeah, yeah," I said. "You already told me that yours is white with black stripes and mine is black with white stripes, but honestly, what's the difference?"

She laughed and admitted she didn't really know.

All the seniors were wearing their togas. Every-thing from prison blues denim to Day-Glo orange, as well as a number of stripes. And, to my surprise, it was fun. Not just wearing the togas and being a senior, but having people I'd gone to school with for years not recognize me. Although I did feel like a deserter when I saw Anna in art class. She seemed lonely.

"How was your China trip?" I asked her, trying to be friendly.

She frowned slightly. "Okay."

"Did you meet any relatives?"

"It really wasn't like that."

"Oh. Yeah, I forgot. You don't really know—"

"No, I don't," Anna said sharply.

I'd never heard Anna talk in *that* kind of voice before. She was always kind to everybody . . . even when people weren't kind to her. Then she said more softly, "I'm surprised you're even talking to me."

"Why?"

"Well, because you're hanging with a new crowd now. And I don't really fit . . ."

I could hear it now . . . the beginning of the martyr tone. So I got mad. "You could if you *wanted* to, Anna," I challenged her. I sounded snippy, but I didn't care. "But you don't even *try* to talk to them."

That one must have hit hard because all of a sudden Anna narrowed her eyes. "Tell me, Kenzie, did your IQ drop when you bleached your hair? Because, if you ask me, you're sounding more and more like a real blonde!" Then she stomped off to sit in the back of the room.

Well. I sighed, attempting to shrug it off as I took a seat near the front. *Whatever.*

I did see Ryun that day, but we just looked at each other without saying a word. I knew that he recognized me, and I suspected he was thinking about what had happened in Virginia. But it was like neither of us knew what to do about it. I figured we'd probably just do nothing.

But the next day, when we ran into each other again, and I was wearing one of the cool outfits I'd gotten while shopping with Sierra, Ryun surprised me by saying, "Hey."

And I said, "Hey." But that was it.

Then I saw him again, and he said, "hey" again.

And I said, "Hey, back." That was when it all started up again. The game continued.

When no one was around to see or hear, Ryun admitted that he'd wanted to call me after Virginia. And then he invited me to do something with him. I mentioned Sierra, and he assured me she'd be busy with yearbook stuff. He was being pretty mysterious about the whole thing, so I couldn't resist.

I had to laugh when we wound up at a tattoo parlor.

"You're kidding?" I said when he parked his Explorer behind it.

He shook his head and took my hand. "Coming?"

"You're getting a tattoo?"

He nodded.

"No way."

"Watch."

And so I helped him decide on a small soccer ball to be applied on his ankle of his kicking foot. He flashed some false ID at the tattoo dude. This guy had about a hundred tattoos all over his arms, chest, and neck. I actually wondered if he practiced his art on himself. But I watched, fascinated, as Ryun sat

there, enduring the pain of the needle injecting
him again and again with the dye. To say I was
impressed was an understatement. I actually considered getting a tattoo too but figured I better pace
myself. My parents hadn't discovered my belly-
button ring yet. No use pushing things.

By the time we got back into Ryun's Explorer,
Ryun and I had another secret. I tried not to think
about what Sierra would say if she knew. But then,
like Ryun said, she didn't *have* to know.

And so we continued, Ryun and me, seeing each
other when we could, snatching up odd moments
like stolen pieces of candy. Watching for times when
Sierra was preoccupied and we were both free. I tried
to convince myself that it was okay. That in time I'd
win Ryun over completely and he'd gracefully break
up with Sierra. Then the right amount of time would
pass, and he and I could go public with our relationship. Because in my heart I believed that Ryun loved
me as much as I loved him.

So why was he still seeing Sierra? The answer
was simple. At least to me and probably to Ryun
too, if he ever admitted it. Ryun and I were sort of
the outsiders of the in crowd. We'd been allowed
in, but only by default, because we knew Sierra. We
both felt insecure and a bit like impostors. It's as if
we'd both created this cool persona that allowed us
passage into their world. But if they ever fully realized what was underneath, they'd quickly throw us
both out. Sometimes I thought that might not be
such a bad thing.

But in the meantime, we both needed someone

kenzie's story

like Sierra to enter the club. She was like the High
High superstar and our ticket to stardom—or at least
to be spectators there. Besides that, we were both
equally fascinated by her. Maybe not her so much
as her money, her incredible taste, her perfect parents, her amazing home, her cool car, and most of
all, her influence. Sierra definitely had influence.

And so, as if by consent, Ryun and I both continued to play this odd little game. If I was perfectly
honest, I'd have to admit that we were both using
Sierra—although there was more to it, at least on
my part. I truly did like her as a person and a
friend. I loved being around her, and I appreciated
her upbeat and cheerful attitude—and her way of
wanting to make each moment a memory. I was
ticked at myself for letting so much of my high
school experience just float by. The three previous
years were just a fuzzy blur. More than anything,
I wanted this, my senior year, to be my best high
school memory ever. And Sierra was a huge part
of that.

And so, when it came to Ryun and me, I was
content to take whatever time I could get, whenever
I could get it, and to simply bide my time. At least
in the beginning.

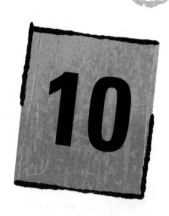

Ryun and I began to have a standing date on Wednesday nights. I'm not even sure what he told Sierra, but she thought he had some family responsibility that kept him busy. And she thought I was at church with my parents since this was the night they took the twins and Lark with them to midweek service. At first my parents, mostly my mom, had protested when I'd refused to come along. Although I have to give them some credit—they might be really into their church and stuff, but at least they don't force their religion down anyone's throat. And after we discussed it civilly, we agreed that since I was almost 18, maybe it was time for me to have my own say in some things.

I was really nervous the first time Ryun came over. Not so much because I thought we'd get caught, although I'm sure that was part of it, but more because I wasn't sure I wanted him to see where I lived. I mean, it's pretty embarrassing.

But I felt a lot better after I gave him the entire theme-house tour, complete with my corny commentary, and he actually thought it was pretty cool.

"Hey, relax, Kenzie," he said. "You should see how my mom decorates."

"What do you mean?" I asked, wondering how anyone as cool as Ryun couldn't live in a totally great house.

"Nah," he said, "you don't want to know."

"Come on," I begged him. "Tell me."

"Okay," he finally said. "It's like Korea meets Kmart. It's like East meets West in this giant collision of plastic and clashing colors. My dad keeps telling my mom that it's okay to buy some real furniture, but it's like she's addicted to those Blue Light Specials or something."

And that's how it went with us. We weren't afraid to be ourselves, to reveal our biggest secrets. Ryun even admitted to me that he drank, sometimes too much.

"But I think it's a stress reliever," he told me. "Everyone puts so much pressure on me with this whole soccer thing. . . . Sometimes I just want to forget the whole thing."

"But you're so great, Ryun. No one plays soccer like you. How could you want to forget that?"

"No, that's not it," he corrected me. "I love soccer. I mean all the pressure people put on me, like about which college to choose, all that . . ."

I nodded. "Yeah, I get that. Sometimes I feel pressure like that in just hanging with—" I stopped myself. I didn't want to say Sierra's name. Not when I was with Ryun. Instead I said, "My new friends."

"I know," he agreed quickly. "That crowd can make me pretty nervous too."

And then we talked about our future, and he promised me that he was going to break it off with Sierra soon.

"But when?" I asked, hoping I didn't sound too pushy.

"It seems like something gets in the way every single time I start to bring it up. It's like Sierra always has something going on that I need to go to or take her to and I keep thinking as soon as we do this or go there, that I will, you know . . ."

And, naturally, I didn't question that. I knew firsthand how persuasive Sierra was. Sometimes it felt like she ran the entire school or, more specifically, our lives.

Slowly the days turned into weeks, and Ryun and I still snatched whatever moments we could get. But more and more I was feeling nervous and sneaky. I was afraid we were going to get caught. Ryun didn't seem worried. But then Ryun was one of those guys who thrived on adventure.

Still, I got seriously jealous every time I saw him and Sierra together. And that was a lot of times, since they had no reason to hide their relationship from anyone. So I was forced to watch and endure— and felt more and more like the loser in this deal.

But it was weird. I didn't always feel bad.

Sometimes my feelings of jealousy and guilt bal-
anced each other out. Most of the time I convinced
myself that everything was okay, that I wasn't doing
anything wrong, and that one of these days it would
all be out in the open and life would go on.

"I can't talk to anyone the way I can talk to you,"
Ryun had told me the night before, when we'd met
at my house. "You make me feel so relaxed." Then
he'd given me a tender kiss.

"I know," I'd told him as I ran my hand through
his silky hair. "I can just be myself around you, and
the rest of the world kind of melts away."

"I wish it could just be you and me, Kenzie,"
he'd told me. "I wish that life was that simple."

But it wasn't simple, I kept reminding myself.
And I had to watch my step around Sierra or it
would get way more complicated.

■   ■   ■

Soon it was Wednesday again, and my family was
just getting ready to go to the midweek service,
although Lark was really putting up a stink. First
she'd tried to convince our parents that she had
homework. Then she'd actually told them she had
cramps, which I knew was a flat-out lie. But I didn't
say anything as I slipped upstairs to escape the fray.

"I don't see why I have to go, but Kenzie doesn't."

"Lark!" Mom was using her warning voice. "You
keep forgetting that Kenzie is almost five years older
than you."

Just then the phone rang and I could hear Lark

answering it. Then she came stomping up the stairs and handed the cordless to me like she'd just climbed Mount Everest to get here. "It's Anna Banana," she said with contempt.

I couldn't believe Anna was calling me, especially since she hadn't said a single word to me since our little blowout in art class when she'd insulted my intelligence *and* my new hair color. But I also knew that Lark should be able to recognize her voice.

"Anna?" I said as I gave Lark a push out of my room and closed the door.

"Hi, Kenzie." Long pause now. "I, uh, just wanted to call and apologize."

"Apologize?" I was getting better and better at playing dumb. Maybe Anna had actually been on to something with her dumb blonde joke.

"You know." I could hear exasperation in her voice now.

"Oh yeah." I flopped down on my bed and waited for her to continue. After all, she'd been the one to call me.

"Well, it wasn't very nice what I said to you that day. And I've felt bad about it. So I wanted to say I'm sorry."

"That's okay," I told her. "It wasn't a big deal."

"So, how are you doing?" she asked.

"Okay, I guess." I could hear the van pulling out of the driveway now.

"I haven't seen you at youth group this year," she continued. "I wondered if you'd like a ride."

Now I *used* to go to youth group on a pretty regular basis with Anna. It was our one big social night out. But the idea of sitting in that stuffy room with all those lame kids now sounded so ridiculous that I thought I might actually laugh, which wouldn't be good. Instead I coughed. "I'm sorry, Anna," I told her in a sober voice. "I've got a lot of homework tonight, and I feel like I'm fighting off some kind of bug."

"Sorry." She paused. "Well, I hope you feel better."

"Thanks." I got up to peek out my window and, sure enough, Ryun was just pulling up.

"I better go," I told her as I headed downstairs.

"Oh yeah," she said, unwilling to let me off the hook just yet. "I thought I'd ask you if you want to invite your *new friends* to youth group next week. We're going to be having a special night, and you know that Carin and Holly both go to church with us."

"Yeah," I told her, eager to get off the phone. "I'll make sure to ask them." And then I told her I really had to go and hung up. But I was thinking, *Yeah, sure, I'll ask them, you bet.* Holly and Carin went to church with their parents sometimes, but neither of those girls had ever set her big toe into a youth group meeting.

"Hey, Ryun," I said as I opened the door with a big smile. Wednesday nights were the highlight of my week. Ryun and I just hanging out and being ourselves. Sometimes I'd play my guitar for him and share some of the songs I'd made up—something I'd never do with anyone else—but mostly we just talked. And we kissed a little. But nothing out of hand because I was always a little on edge, worried that my parents would suddenly come home early one night. But, thankfully, that hadn't happened yet. Basically we just had a good time, and I think we both enjoyed it. Wednesday was my happy day.

■   ■   ■

I knew by the end of September that I was in trouble. Oh, not serious trouble, I guess—I certainly wasn't pregnant! But I was in financial trouble, which was actually quite serious considering the spending habits of my new friends. My shopping sprees over the past few months had almost completely drained my savings account. I'd managed to spend thousands of dollars. Okay, it wasn't like tens of thousands, but it was more than three! It wasn't like I regretted all the beautiful shoes and clothes I'd purchased—no, not at all. I simply regretted the balance on my savings account statement that month. In fact, I gasped when I read it.

"What's wrong?" asked my mom as she sorted through the rest of the mail.

"Oh, nothing." I slipped the envelope into my back pocket and forced a smile.

"Money problems?" She eyed me carefully. "I've noticed you've been spending more than usual lately."

I swallowed and nodded. "I know, Mom. But it's my money, right?"

"Of course, honey. But you've always been such a good saver."

"Well, it's my senior year, Mom. I just wanted to have a good time."

She frowned slightly, then seemed to think of something. "But it's going to be hard to continue having a good time if you're broke."

I shrugged. "Yeah, maybe . . ."

"Well, there's always room for you at Little Lambs."

"I know . . ."

"The kids miss you, honey. Blain keeps asking when Kenny is coming back."

I smiled. "Oh, Blain."

And so I hatched a new plan. I actually wrote it into a proposal that I handed over to my mom that same day. "I want to be taken seriously," I told her as I gave her the freshly printed sheet.

"PE, music, and art instructor." She read some more, then nodded. "This is quite good, Kenzie."

"Yeah," I said eagerly. "I got to thinking . . . I only need to go half days from here on out to graduate, but the idea of just filling in at Little Lambs feels, well, sort of demeaning, you know. But I was thinking if I had a *real* title and job description—"

"And *raise?*" My mom adjusted her glasses as she read the bottom line. "You want *10 dollars an hour?*"

"That's really not that much," I began. "Most people make a whole lot more than—"

"Not in day care." She put down the paper and studied me.

"But I'd be like a specialist. I'd do lesson plans

and everything. Think about it, Mom. It'd really make your afternoons go so much more smoothly," I tried to convince her. "And besides, you're always talking about enrichment. Music, art, PE—how much more enrichment can you get?"

She smiled. "You make a good point."

"I already have a lot of arts and crafts ideas from working at camp. And for PE I thought I could begin teaching them soccer. I might even bring in a real expert." Of course, I was thinking about Ryun. "And for music, I will bring my guitar and—"

"Okay, okay, honey. You've convinced me."

I grinned. "Really?"

"Absolutely. Now, do you think you can convince the board?"

I considered this. Little Lambs has had a board since the beginning. It was the church's way of making sure the day care didn't get out of control. "I think so."

"All right," she said. "I'll give them a call and get this set up for you."

■   ■   ■

I went before the board the following week. Dressed in my most "professional" outfit, a navy skirt and crisp white shirt, I stood before them and talked with enthusiasm about the children and what I'd like to do.

"This is marvelous," said Mrs. Trent.

"If only more young people would take such initiative," said another.

88

And when put to the vote, it was unanimous. I was their new art, music, and PE teacher, and I would be working from 1:00 to 5:30 daily for 10 dollars an hour.

"Congratulations," my mom proudly told me.

"Thanks." I grinned, mentally calculating my next paycheck's earnings. "When do I begin?"

"Tomorrow."

"Cool." And it wasn't just the money, although that was a nice incentive. I really was looking forward to being with the kids again. But not just as their overgrown playmate this time. This time I'd have something concrete to offer them, and I liked that. I also knew I wouldn't be missing out on too much with my friends since most of them had after-school activities in various clubs that kept them busy until around 5:00 anyway. Plus, I still had weekends free.

Ryun was the first one I called with the good news. We talked a lot on the phone during those days. It was a safe, simple, and inexpensive way to spend time together. "I'm hoping you'll be able to come in sometime," I told him. "To give them a few soccer tips. I'm sure they'll be impressed."

"No problem. Just tell me when and where."

But on the day I wanted Ryun to stop by and teach some soccer skills, he had other plans. And when I discovered it was to go shoe shopping with Sierra, I was a little jealous. Okay, *very* jealous. I was jealous that Sierra had invited Ryun instead of me, even though I wouldn't have been able to go. And I was jealous that Ryun would rather go look at

degrees of betrayal

stupid shoes than come and give deprived children some soccer tips. Even though he reassured me that he'd come any other time, it still hurt.

And it got me to thinking. What kind of game was I really playing here? And who was the real loser? I mean, Sierra and Ryun got to go around in public as a couple while I had to sneak and lurk in the shadows until it was time for Ryun to throw a scrap of affection my way. How fair was that?

So when Taylor Hatfield turned on the charm the next day, the same way he'd been trying to get my attention for the past couple of weeks, I actually paused and took notice. Not only that, but I tossed it right back.

"Now *that's* what I'm talking about," said Taylor with a broad grin as he sat down beside me at the lunch table. "I didn't think you were ever going to give me the time of day, Kenzie."

I smiled at him. "I guess I'm just a slow starter."

He nodded. "Hey, babe, a slow starter usually burns hotter."

"Whoa," said Holly, laughing and elbowing me. "Better control yourself, Taylor."

"Hey, I've been waiting for weeks to get Kenzie to talk to me."

"Yeah," teased Carin, "she's turned into such a snob."

"Have not," I defended myself.

"Well, that's all in the past," said Taylor. "Kenzie and I are going to have a fresh new start now. Right, Kenzie?"

I felt Ryun's eyes on me, but I didn't care. I guess

I was just tired of being on the losing end of our little game. "That's right, Taylor."

So that's when Taylor Hatfield and I became an item. And by the end of the day it was old news.

"Why do you want to go out with a football jock?" Ryun asked me on the phone that night.

"Why not?"

"He just doesn't seem like your type, Kenzie."

"And *my type* would be?"

"Me, of course."

I laughed. "Maybe. But you seem to have your hands full with Sierra at the moment."

"Does that mean you're giving up on me, Kenzie?"

"Why would I give up on you, Ryun?" I could hear the teasing note in my voice, but I didn't really care. Let Ryun be in my shoes for a change.

"Things are going to change," he said quietly.

"Things always do," I tossed right back.

Before I knew it, I was going out with Taylor in public but still secretly seeing Ryun on the side. It was all pretty amazing. One short year ago neither of these boys would've given me a second look, and now they couldn't get enough of me. I did feel a tiny bit guilty about Taylor since he was acting totally devoted to me. He even brought me a rose one day. But at the same time I knew he didn't have the best reputation for loyalty to his girlfriends anyway, so I figured, *Hey, what goes around comes around.*

Besides, he was fun—always the life of the party after football games or whatever. It was exciting

being Taylor's girl. Did I love him? Not at all. But
what did love have to do with having a good time?
And what good did love do if the guy you loved was
dating someone else?

11

Taylor and I lasted all of one month. And in some ways I really liked the guy. Unfortunately, at least in his mind, I didn't like him enough to sleep with him. And eventually I got tired of his pressure. Just days before the last big game of the year I decided to call it quits.

"You broke up with Taylor Hatfield?" demanded Holly as she gave me a ride to Little Lambs after school. "Why?"

"He's too pushy," I told her.

"But he actually brought you flowers last week."

"Yeah, that was sweet."

"I don't get it, Kenzie. That guy was absolutely in love with you."

I laughed. "He was in love with the idea of getting me into bed."

"Oh."

"Yeah. And I just wasn't into that."

She parked in front of Little Lambs and peered into the cluttered play yard. "You really like working here?"

"Yeah." I grabbed my bag. "These kids are great. And really smart too. It's pretty fun teaching them new things."

She didn't look convinced.

"Hey, you want to come in and meet some of them?" I offered suddenly.

She looked down at her shoes, then frowned. "No, thanks."

Actually I was slightly relieved since I knew that meeting my mother would be unavoidable if Holly came in. "Another time," I said lightly as I got out.

"Yeah, another time," she echoed.

I was thinking, *Yeah, sure,* as I waved and shut the door. *Another lifetime maybe.* Holly never came out here and neither did Sierra. Too many other *important* things to do. It wasn't that I held things like this against anyone. I just didn't get it. I mean, I like pretty shoes as much as the next girl—well, other than Sierra, that is—but shoes are just *things.* Shoes will wear out or go out of style or trip you up and break your ankle, and kids, well, they are something else altogether.

For the sake of my friends and for Taylor, I acted like I was pretty down about the breakup. "I guess it just wasn't working," I told Sierra later.

"I'm sorry," she said, looking sad. Then she frowned. "He's such a jerk to break up with you— and right before the game on Friday too."

I didn't even mind that she assumed he was the one to break it off. It just made things simpler and kept the sympathy factor in my court. The only person who seemed really glad about the breakup was Ryun. And I wasn't sure whether that was a good thing or not.

"Smart move," he told me after school. He had offered me a ride to Little Lambs since Sierra had an emergency student council meeting, something to do with the last game, and Holly was busy with cheerleading practice. And Ryun used this opportunity to spend time with me. We were out in the school parking lot, sitting in his Explorer.

"Yeah, I guess."

"Then why do you seem so down?"

"I don't know . . ." I looked out the passenger-side window and sighed. I really wanted to tell him that I was sad because the only guy I really cared about was dating somebody else. But instead I stayed quiet.

I felt his hand on my shoulder and turned to see him peering at me, his dark eyes burning holes down into my soul. "It won't be forever, Kenzie." Then he reached over, pulled me toward him, and held me tightly. "Just be patient, okay?"

I held on to him and wished more than anything that we could just stay like this forever. I started crying then, but Ryun just gently wiped my tears away. "Really, it won't be much longer, Kenzie."

"How long will it be?" I pulled away and sniffed.

"I don't know."

"Right." I turned and looked out the window again as he started the ignition and pulled out of the parking lot.

All right, maybe I was totally stupid to spend any more time with him, like it was just an open invitation for pain. Maybe I needed to just cut off Ryun Lee, cold turkey, end this thing like a bad habit. But as I turned and looked at him, ready to speak my piece, to tell him to just forget the whole thing and to never call or talk to me again, I stopped. I watched him intently looking at the road, his brow creased with concern as a stray lock of sleek black hair hung into his beautiful dark eyes. And suddenly I remembered how I felt in his arms. Oh, crud, how could I not love this guy?

I enjoyed the newfound sympathy I got from my friends during the next couple of days. Poor Taylor had "miraculously" recovered from his broken heart and started dating Tiffany Powers the same week. Now everyone was talking about it, playing it out like I was the victim. It didn't hurt that no one liked Tiffany Powers very much.

It was funny how the tables could turn in our little group. It was like we always needed someone to play hero or villain—and everything was either black or white. I guess it would've been too boring to just let people simply live their lives and make decisions without having everyone second-guessing them. Just the same, I didn't mind having a bit of the limelight for a change.

"Taylor's such a player," said Carin as we stood in the hallway. "He was acting all hurt over you and

now he's already hooked up with stupid Tiffany.
I saw them making out in the locker bay."

"Really?" I tried to act shocked and hurt. "And
I was actually having second thoughts about getting
back with him."

"Really?"

I shrugged. "I don't know."

"Well, it's settled," said Sierra with conviction.
"You are coming to the game with me tonight."

I looked at her in surprise. "Really?"

"Yes, and I won't take no for an answer."

I'd just assumed that Sierra and Ryun would
be going to the game together tonight and that
I would be going alone or staying home, which
might be preferable to going to the game by
myself. But now I wondered if Ryun was going
to do the breakup dance with Sierra. Or maybe
he already had.

I imagined that Ryun and I would finally be
free to be together. It might do a little damage
to my friendship with Sierra, at least temporarily,
but I had seen lots of other friendships survive
those things before. It just seemed to be an
accepted thing in high school. You liked someone
one day and broke up the next. Everyone talked
about it for a few days, and then they moved on
to the next juicy bit of scandal. No big deal, really.

So I agreed to go to the game with Sierra. As I
zipped up coats at Little Lambs, I imagined how we'd
have a girls' night out. And how maybe I'd have to
comfort her over her breakup with Ryun. But I'd be
prepared for her heartache. I'd tell her what a truly

great person she was and how Ryun was a total fool not to appreciate her—stuff like that.

I was surprised when she showed up in her dad's classic '57 Chevy.

"Hop in," she called through the open passenger door.

Sierra looked great, as usual, every hair in place and wearing what looked like a new sweater and matching Skechers in our school color of royal purple.

"Nice outfit," I told her.

When I noticed she wasn't heading toward the school, I asked, "Where are you going?"

"To get Ryun."

"You never told—"

"Because if I had, you wouldn't have come. And you need to be at this game tonight, Kenzie. It's the last football game of our senior year."

I tuned her out as she began to ramble on about how we were making memories. . . . If only she knew the memories I'd already made this year— with her boyfriend. And now this! But before I could think of an excuse to be dropped off at the next corner, we were picking up Ryun.

"I'm sorry," Sierra said sweetly as she waved at him. "I should've told you that Ryun was coming. But I knew that you wouldn't have come."

Ryun looked a little surprised to see me too. I got out of the car so he could sit in the front seat next to Sierra.

"Don't worry about it, Kenzie," she said. "It's okay, really. Ryun and I are kind of like an old married couple now." She glanced at him and giggled. "And it'll be fun having you along, Kenzie."

"I don't know . . ."

"Come on, don't spoil this night," she pleaded.

"But I—"

"Come on," she urged. "We can all sit in the front seat."

So I got in and, feeling like a total fool, turned and looked out the side window as I longed for this evening to end. I wished I hadn't come and even considered pretending like I was sick and calling home and begging Mom or Dad to pick me up. But then, once I was at the game and I heard the band playing and saw our team down on the field, well, I guess I got caught up in the whole thing. After all, it was time to make a memory, right?

Then, just as halftime began and the marching band took the field, Holly came up to the bleachers and whispered in my ear, "Is it true?"

I looked at her. "Huh?"

"Come on," she said suddenly. "We need to use the bathroom."

"But I don't really have to—" Too late, she was already tugging me down the bleachers toward the bathroom.

"What are you talking about?" I demanded as we clomped down the stairs.

"About you and Ryun Lee."

A wave of shock ran through me, but I tried to appear unrattled. "What do you mean?"

"I saw you and Ryun in the parking lot the other day."

"He gave me a ride to work."

"That's not all." Holly pulled me into the bathroom with her, then went into the stall at the far end. I went into the stall next to her and continued to talk.

"What do you mean?" I was thankful for the privacy of the stall now because I knew the look on my face had to be a dead giveaway.

"I *mean* a lot of things make sense now, Kenzie. You and Ryun have *something* going on. Don't lie to me."

I groaned and leaned my head against the door.

"So, it's true?" she asked.

"I don't know," I muttered.

"Meaning, *yes?*"

"He told me he's going to break up with her," I began hopelessly. "I'm just waiting for it to happen."

"You need to tell Sierra what's going on, Kenzie."

"I—I can't do—"

"Look, I know you don't want to upset Sierra," she said. "But she's a big girl. She can handle it."

"Tell Ryun that. He's so afraid of hurting her."

"So you're just going to keep seeing each other behind Sierra's back?"

"I don't know what we're going to do." I felt completely trapped now. "It's just that . . ." I groped for the right words. "Ryun and I connect on a deep level, deeper than he and Sierra ever could."

"What do you mean?"

"Ryun is so real, so deep. He's just not rah-rah like Sierra. Don't get me wrong. I really like Sierra. She's a lot of fun. Ryun really likes her too. That's what makes this so hard. Neither of us wants to hurt her feelings, you know?"

"You have to tell her. Get it out in the open." I heard the toilet flush and her stall door opening. I knew I had to go out there and face her.

I stepped out and looked at Holly. "I just don't know how to—"

"You've got to do something, Kenzie." She was checking her hair now and reapplying some lip gloss.

"I know. I know." I just stood there and stared. My life was unraveling before my very eyes.

"And the sooner the better," she said in a firm voice. We looked at each other in the mirror, and I suddenly got the feeling that I was letting her down. "In the meantime I'll try to run damage control," she told me. "But you better prepare yourself for the worst-case scenario if word gets out before you and Ryun break the news to Sierra."

"Oh, Holly." I closed my eyes and leaned forward on the sink. What a mess.

"Now don't start freaking. That'll be a dead give-away." She pulled me up and made me stand up straight. "Hold your head up high. And if anybody asks about it, just deny everything."

"Really?"

"It's the only way."

"All right." I lifted my chin and forced a smile. "Thanks."

"Just watch your step tonight."

Then I walked back to the stands and sat down, acting like nothing was wrong. But at the same time it felt like something had changed in my world. I couldn't even put my finger on it for sure, but it seemed like Sierra was a little agitated during the second half. Maybe she was just excited about the close score since it was the last game of our senior year and we were supposed to be making a memory tonight.

Yet at the same time I felt as if my own memory was being wiped clean that night. I was so stressed about being at the game with the two of them. I knew the word could be getting out about Ryun and me . . . how I was such a horrible friend for cheating on my best friend with her boyfriend.

The entire second half of the game floated by me in this hazy slow motion—sort of surreal and weird. I was so thankful when the final horn blew. Apparently our team had won because everyone was happy. And at last we were working our way through the crowd and down the steps of the stadium.

"Let's get pizza," Ryun said when the game ended.

"Fine," Sierra said. But she sounded mad.

I looked over at her, and she just glared at me. *Uh-oh.* I turned quickly to ask Holly and Carin, "Are you guys . . . ?"

"No!" Sierra said sharply. "Just us. Let's go." And then she walked away.

"What gives?" Ryun asked me.

"Don't know," I said. But my heart was pounding. Did Sierra *know?* Could she have heard about Ryun and me or figured it out?

Sierra was already sitting in her dad's car when

Ryun and I got there. As soon as we got in, Sierra drove away from the stadium without saying anything. But I knew she was upset—she almost hit a light pole on the way out of the parking lot.

Before long the silence in that car became so thick and heavy that I found it difficult to breathe.

Sierra was heading down Route 58 now, but I could tell by the way she was driving, recklessly and going way too fast, that something was wrong. Seriously wrong. And that's when the stuff hit the fan. And, man-oh-man, did it ever get ugly in there!

12

It wasn't supposed to happen like this. But I didn't know what to do or how to stop what was already in motion. Like this big hulking car the three of us were in, flying down Route 58 in the middle of the night—heading somewhere that no one wanted to go. I seriously wished I could just vanish as I clung to the edge of the car seat. Why had I even come along tonight?

We were still in Sierra's dad's car, but at least Ryun was driving now. That was a relief since I felt sure Sierra was going to kill all three of us if she'd kept driving like a madwoman. But then finally she pulled over and ran away from the car. Ryun followed her, trying to sort this mess out. Fat chance. Some things just aren't fixable. And this was one of them.

Now Sierra was slumped over on my right, lean-ing into the passenger door and just sobbing. *That* was really getting to me. I was *supposed* to be her best friend, and she'd done so much for me this year. *And this is how I repay her?* I thought. *How can I even stand myself?*

Ryun was driving in silence, both hands gripping the wheel, going as fast as he could without risking a ticket. I knew he felt horrible too. Everything was just all wrong tonight—out of control—and none of us knew how to make it right again.

"I'm *sorry*, Sierra," I said for like the hundredth time. "Really, I never meant for this—"

"Sorry?" She practically spit out the word as she sat up straight and faced me. Even in the dim light of the console, I could see her eyes were angry and her face was still wet with tears. "That's *all* you can say, McKenzie Parker?"

When she clenched her fists, I was afraid she was actually going to hit me. I knew I deserved it.

"You guys are total traitors! Liars! Cheaters! And all you can say is a pathetic little *'I'm sorry'*?" She slammed her fist into the dashboard. "I hate you both! And I won't spend another second with you!"

And then, as Ryun was driving almost 60 miles an hour, Sierra reached for the door handle and started to open the passenger door.

"Sierra!" I screamed. *"No!"* Certain she was going to jump, I grabbed on to her left arm with both hands at the same time Ryun reached across me to grab on to her as well—and then it was too late.

First the car swung to the right. I could hear gravel grinding beneath the tires, and I knew we were headed straight for the ditch. I clung to Sierra and prayed. In that same instant, Ryun jerked the steering wheel sharply to the left, and we began to careen back onto the highway but at an odd angle. That was when the car started to spin. And, like the carnival rides I used to love, we flipped, then went sideways, over and over. Only this time no one was buckled into place, and we were tossed and thrown like crash-test dummies until the car finally came to a dead halt, upside down.

I heard Ryun groan in pain as he pushed the driver's-side door open. "We gotta get outta here," he said, reaching for my arm. It seemed to take forever for us to crawl out of the crumpled car. And that was when I noticed that Sierra wasn't getting out. She wasn't even moving.

"Sierra!" I shrieked. "Ryun, we have to get Sierra out!" I could tell that he was hurt. I thought it was his leg. But acting as his crutch, I managed to help him to the other side of the car where Sierra was trapped between the front and back seats. As we jerked and pulled to get the crunched door open, something made an exploding sound from the engine.

"Hurry!" I yelled at Ryun. "I think it's going to blow up!"

We tugged on Sierra and finally managed to extract her from the mangled car seats. Smoke was everywhere now. Together we dragged her limp body about 30 feet from the car just as another explosion occurred and the '57 Chevy burst into flames. I was sure she was dead. And equally sure it was all my fault.

"Sierra!" I sobbed, bending over her. "Sierra, say something, please." I put my face close to hers. She was breathing, but blood was coming from her head, so I knew this was serious. I realized she only had on a sweater, the new purple one she'd gotten just for the game tonight. So I removed my hooded sweatshirt and laid it over her. For the second time tonight and the first time in months, I prayed.

The trip to the hospital was a blur of flashing lights and sirens and uniforms. A few preliminary questions were asked, but Sierra was still unconscious, and Ryun and I were both too rattled to think straight. Fortunately the emergency crew quickly assessed that, of the three of us, Sierra was in the most danger, so she was the first one they loaded up and whisked away. Ryun and I followed in the second ambulance. His face was pale and his features tight as they loaded his stretcher into the back. He didn't say a word. I insisted that I was okay and perfectly able to walk. Even so, they treated me as if I were injured. Once we were at the hospital I was carefully examined by a woman doctor with a gentle voice.

"You kids had quite a night," she said as she removed her cold stethoscope from my back.

I nodded, swallowing the lump in my throat. "Do you know how Sierra Reynolds is doing?"

"Not yet. But don't worry. Your friend is in good hands." The doctor was writing something on her chart now. "You're a lucky girl, McKenzie."

I wanted to ask her what she meant by that, but instead I kept my mouth shut.

"You all could've been killed tonight."

"I know," I said solemnly.

"Looks like all you've got are a lot of bruises and abrasions." She smiled. "I'd recommend some extra-strength Tylenol and a few ice packs."

"Thanks," I mumbled. "Can I get dressed now?"

"Sure. I think your parents are in the waiting area."

I felt like I'd been run over by a truck as I pulled on my jeans and T-shirt. I didn't know where my sweatshirt was, and even though it was fairly new I didn't even care. I shoved my feet into my dusty Doc Martens and noticed that there was a smear of blood on the right toe. I wasn't sure whose blood it was, but I suspected it was Sierra's and I wanted it to be gone. I got a paper towel and attempted to wipe it off. But it was already dry, and I had to spit on the paper towel and really scrub before it finally disappeared.

I felt slightly dizzy as I stood up, and I wondered if I'd hit my head during the wreck. But I couldn't seem to find a lump. In some ways, I thought it would've been better if I *had* been hurt. Like maybe that would somehow make up for everything. Mostly I just wished I could turn back the clock and do it all differently.

I noticed a mirror above the wastebasket, but the image I saw looked like someone else. I stepped closer and peered at the person I no longer knew. Who was this girl who had lied to her parents and betrayed her best friend? What had I become? I reached up and fingered a strand of long hair. The golden highlights I paid 50 bucks to have done every other month looked cheap and brassy in the harsh fluorescent light, and in spite of my weekly trip to the tanning salon, my skin appeared sallow and unhealthy. I grabbed a tissue and attempted to remove the ugly black smudges beneath my eyes—ruined mascara, a result of all the crying I'd been doing. Although I wasn't seriously injured by the accident, I felt like a total wreck. And I still wondered how it had all happened.

The fluorescent lamp made an irritating buzzing noise as I stood there in the examining room and attempted to gather my bearings. I wasn't ready to face my parents yet. I didn't know how I was going to explain all this to them. How could I make them understand? I wasn't even sure I understood it myself. In fact, I felt pretty foggy about everything, and I actually wished I'd suffered a head injury that could produce amnesia. No such luck.

I braced myself as I walked slowly through the shadows of the hallway toward the more brightly lit waiting area. First I saw Ryun's parents. Sitting across from the receptionist's desk, Ryun's father had one arm around the shoulders of the tiny woman that I knew was Mrs. Lee. She was bent over, hugging her purse to her middle as she cried softly. Then,

standing off by themselves, were Sierra's parents.
As always, they were perfectly dressed. They looked
slightly out of place in the no-frills waiting area.
I could tell by their expressions that they were worried about their daughter, but even so they both
stood straight and tall. If I hadn't seen their faces,
I might've assumed they were attending a social
function.

Then I spotted my parents sitting over by the
window. They didn't see me yet. And for a moment,
I was reminded of how they really do resemble the
parents on the old sitcom *Roseanne*. Lark had been
the first one to point out this oddity to me. Ever since
my dad had installed cable this year (against my
mom's better judgment) Lark had become addicted
to the channel that ran the old family sitcoms. And
Roseanne was by far her favorite. I figured this was
due to the family resemblance. The dad on the show
was a contractor—our dad was a contractor. The
parents on the show were both frumpy and over-
weight—our parents were both frumpy and over-
weight. Even the birth order of the kids was similar,
except that instead of one little brother, we had two.

But that's where the comparisons ended. Whereas
the sitcom family was loud, sarcastic, and comfortable using what my mom would call "language," the
Parkers were a churchgoing family, relatively quiet,
and conservative. In fact, my parents were really
loving and generous, almost to a fault. After observing my other friends' parents, I'd actually wondered
if my parents gave *too* much.

For instance, my dad had spent the last five years

building "affordable" homes on a parcel of land that he'd purchased and developed himself. But because he was so generous, he barely made wages on a project that could've made us millionaires. Then, of course, there was my mom and her do-good efforts at Little Lambs. My folks were nice enough people, I'd been thinking, but they never seemed to get ahead financially.

But tonight as I saw my rather ordinary parents sitting in the uncomfortable plastic chairs in the waiting area, I didn't see them in this same negative light. Yeah, I knew my mom looked like the aging hippie she was in her long faded denim jumper over an old tie-dyed T-shirt. And I couldn't imagine what Sierra would say if she saw Mom's footwear— her rolled-down cotton socks were shoved into a decrepit pair of Birkenstocks that were even older than me. Plus, my mom's hair had gone naturally and unfashionably gray and she never cut it. Instead she braided it and twisted it into some sort of bun, then secured it with a couple of plastic chopsticks. And then there was my dad—in his usual uniform of plaid flannel shirt and Wrangler jeans that tend to ride low, and not in a fashionable way. And as usual he was wearing his heavy black boots, not Doc Martens either, but ones with steel toes designed to protect him from falling two-by-fours. Nothing could be more opposite from Sierra's totally cool parents. And yet I was so very glad to see them. And even though Sierra's parents had never met them— because I'd never allowed any of my new friends, most of all Sierra, to meet them, I no longer cared.

"Mom, Dad," I said as I rushed toward them.

They both got up as one and greeted me with arms opened wide. I was quickly swallowed into their big warm hug. Finally their embrace relaxed, and we all stepped back and looked at each other. I could tell by my mom's red-rimmed eyes that she'd been crying, and my dad looked about 20 years older.

"I'm so glad you're okay, honey," said Mom as she fished in her pocket for a tissue to wipe her nose.

"We were so worried," said Dad. "We were coming home from the Scout jamboree this evening when we saw all the ambulances and police cars heading out Route 58." He shook his head. "We had no idea it was for you kids. How are the others?"

"I—uh—I don't know. I mean, Ryun isn't so bad. Although his leg seems to be injured. But—but—" I started to sob now. "I'm not—not sure about Sierra. She was hurt pretty badly and I—" I choked on my words. "I thought she was dead. But she wasn't."

My parents led me over to where they'd been sitting, and we all sat down in a little triangle. They asked me to tell them exactly what happened since the details had been sketchy so far. I was ready to open up and simply pour out the whole awful story, including all the horrible details of how Ryun and I were sneaking around behind Sierra's back and how she found out. I wanted to tell my parents the complete truth, and I never wanted to lie to them again about anything. But then I heard someone calling my name.

"McKenzie Parker?" called the woman from the reception desk for a second time.

"You better go see what it is, honey," said my mom as we all stood up together and headed for the desk.

"Are you McKenzie Parker?" asked the receptionist.

I nodded.

"Ryun Lee is requesting to see you," she said, jerking her thumb over her shoulder. "He's just back from X-ray and waiting for the doctor to come give him the results. He's in examining area 5."

I sensed Ryun's parents stirring behind me now. I was sure they were looking my way, wondering why I was being asked to go see their son instead of them.

"You better go, honey," said my mom.

"Don't stay more than five minutes," warned the receptionist.

"Okay," I answered, feeling nervous. I turned to my parents. "I'll be right back."

"Tell him that we're praying for him," said my mother with concerned eyes.

14

I hurried back into the emergency room where I'd recently been examined and quickly located Ryun. He was on the examining bed with his eyes closed.

"Ryun?" I said quietly, unwilling to disturb him.

"Kenzie." He opened his eyes and reached out for me.

I stepped closer, took his hand, and held it tightly. "How're you doing?"

He groaned. "I've been better."

"Your parents are here."

He nodded. "I know."

"Have you heard anything about Sierra?"

Without answering my question, he glanced over my shoulder, then lowered his voice. "Have the police talked to you yet?"

"You mean since we got to the hospital?"

"Yeah. You didn't really say much at the accident. Did you?"

"No. All I could think about was getting Sierra some help."

"Well, they've been in to question me."

"Why?"

"Oh, you know, the regular stuff. Like, had we been drinking or anything."

"But we hadn't."

"I know. And I told them."

I knew Ryun was getting at something, but I wasn't sure what. "And?"

"Look, Kenzie, they think Sierra was driving."

It took a moment for this to sink in. "You told them that *Sierra* was driving?" I frowned now. "But why?"

"I didn't tell them she was driving. I just didn't tell them she *wasn't*. So just don't volunteer any information, okay?" His hand clung to mine, like I was his lifeline. I knew I could deny him nothing.

I nodded but then asked, "Why?"

"I'll be in serious trouble if they find out I was driving tonight. Remember—my license got suspended after homecoming."

I remembered. Other than Asher, Ryun's coach, I was the only one who knew.

"But the accident wasn't your fault," I said. I was actually thinking it was Sierra's fault. After all, she was the one who had tried to open the door and jump. And yet I knew that wasn't right either. She wouldn't have wanted to jump under normal circumstances. If I were honest, I'd have to admit that it was really *my* fault. But I was too afraid to say it. I didn't want to hear those words out loud.

"It doesn't matter *whose* fault it was," said Ryun in a tired voice. "What happened happened. We just need to pick up the pieces and do the best we can now."

"But what about—?" I choked on her name again. "What about Sierra?"

He pressed his lips tightly together, as if he knew something.

"What?" I asked him. *"What is it?"*

"Shh. Keep your voice down."

"But what are you saying?" I demanded in a quiet but strained voice. "Did you hear something about Sierra? Is she—is she not going to—?"

"She's still alive, Kenzie. At least I think so."

My knees got weak, and I leaned on his bed for support. "Oh, Ryun," I groaned. "What if she dies?"

"A nurse said that she's in a coma and that she's probably suffered serious brain damage. She said that Sierra may never gain consciousness again . . . or if she does she might always be in a vegetative state."

I felt my eyes growing wide. "The nurse told you *that?*"

"She didn't tell me. I overheard her talking to another nurse while I was waiting to go to X-ray."

"Oh no." Fresh tears slipped down my cheeks. "I can't—can't believe it."

"I know, Kenzie. It's horrible." He reached for my

hand again. "The doctor told me that we all could've been killed."

"Oh no," I sobbed. "Poor Sierra."

"Excuse me," said a feminine voice. I turned to see the doctor who had examined me coming in now. She was looking at me as if it was time to go.

"I'll see you later, Ryun," I said as I released his hand. Then I remembered. "My mom said to tell you she's praying for you."

"Tell her thanks."

As I left the room, I replayed Ryun's words through my head. *"Sierra's in a coma . . . may never regain consciousness . . . a vegetative state."* It just seemed so unreal, so unbelievable. How did this happen? As I stepped back out into the hallway, I saw Ryun's parents coming in. This time his mom looked up to me with hopeful eyes. I paused to tell them that I just saw Ryun, that it looked like he was doing much better. The doctor was probably telling him the results of the X-ray right now.

"Thank you," said his father.

His mother nodded with appreciation in her eyes.

I noticed that Sierra's parents were no longer standing by the reception area. When my parents came to join me, I asked them where the Reynolds went.

"The doctor came out," my mom explained. "He said they're moving Sierra up to ICU. Apparently she was still unconscious. He told her parents they could use the waiting room up there."

"Did he say anything else?"

Mom shook her head. "I feel so bad that I haven't

had a chance to get to know her or her parents. Dad and I have been so busy this fall—"

"It's not your fault," I assured her. "I've been busy too."

"But at least we've met Ryun," said Dad. "And we introduced ourselves to his parents."

I nodded. "That's good."

"The policeman was here while you were in with Ryun," Dad continued. "He said he needs to ask you a few questions."

I glanced around but didn't see any uniformed officers anywhere. "Where did he go?"

"He needed to speak to the Reynolds about something," Mom put in.

"I gave him our address and phone number," Dad added. "He said he'll contact you at home if he doesn't catch you tonight."

My mom checked her watch. "Do you want to go home now, honey?"

Not sure what I should do, I glanced nervously around the deserted waiting area. "I don't know. I hate to leave my friends here. I don't know what's going to happen. . . ." My head was beginning to throb.

"You've been through a lot tonight," Mom said. "I think you should go home and get some rest."

"But what about Sierra? What if—?" My voice cracked at the thought of her not making it. "She's in bad shape. I can't just leave her."

"There's nothing you can do for her," my dad said.

"Except pray," my mom added.

"I know, but . . ."

"Come on, honey," Mom urged. "We should get you home."

I couldn't think of any other argument so, feeling about five years old, I let the two of them lead me to my mom's big old blue van, the one she used for the day-care kids. I slowly climbed inside, aching with each step. I collapsed into the middle seat and sobbed into an old beach towel that was covering the seat. My mom sat down beside me. She ran her hands through my hair, just like she used to do when I was little. And then she told me quietly, again and again, "It'll be okay."

But this time I knew she was wrong. Nothing was ever going to be okay again.

Our house looked sturdy and comforting as my dad pulled into our well-lit driveway. I'd finally stopped crying. As I looked up at the white Cape Cod, I felt like I hadn't been there in ages. Almost as if I'd already gone off to college and was just coming back for the first time. I guess it was because my more-active-than-usual social life had kept me busy.

My parents helped me from the van, and I distracted myself from the pain in every muscle and joint as I studied the lines of our traditional house and neatly landscaped yard. It wasn't so bad really. I never worried too much about having my cool friends pick me up or drop me off in front of the house. I just never wanted them to come inside, didn't want them to see the theme house. But tonight it seemed warm and friendly and welcoming. Had it changed? Or just me?

My mom helped me get into bed, and my dad

brought me a plate of oatmeal-raisin cookies and a tall glass of milk.

"Your mom made these before we went to the Scout jamboree," he told me as he set them on my bedside table. "I guess she was thinking of you." My dad put his arm around her shoulders.

I studied the two of them standing there. Frumpy but cute. I felt guilty that I'd wasted so much time and energy comparing them to Sierra's parents. I knew who I'd rather come home to, who I'd rather have hugging me. Especially when I felt so confused about everything.

"Don't you want to try one?" My dad held the plate of cookies in front of me and smiled hopefully. I took a cookie and pretended to take a nibble. But my stomach was still in knots and I couldn't eat.

"Want to talk about it?" my mom asked.

"I'm tired," I said, which wasn't a lie. But the truth was, I didn't want to talk about it yet. Not to anyone. I needed to think about what Ryun and I were going to do. But just then my head felt muddled, and I wondered again if I hadn't gotten some sort of concussion after all. I mean, how could you roll around in a car and get whacked about like that without having your brains seriously rattled?

"I just want to go to sleep," I told my parents, closing my eyes and wishing that the world would go away.

My mom pushed the hair back from my face, then leaned over and kissed me on the cheek. "That's a good idea, honey. You go to sleep and we'll talk in the morning."

"Good night, Mouse," said my dad.

I nodded without opening my eyes and listened as they walked across the room and turned out the light. They left my door open a crack, the way they used to do when I was sick with the flu or something, but I didn't get up to close it. I just lay there, wondering how I got into this mess.

I woke up in pain. Every inch of my body hurt, and I couldn't remember why. Then it came back to me. *The wreck.* The sun was barely up and the digital by my bed said it wasn't even eight o'clock, and this wasn't a school day. I felt like I'd been lying on a torture rack. It was painful to crawl out of bed, but I knew it would feel better to be up.

I groaned as I pulled on my sweats. I could see the dark coloration of bruises beginning to appear on my arms and legs, a purplish black growing just beneath the surface of my skin. I couldn't believe I didn't break anything. I wondered about Sierra and Ryun as I pulled my hair back into a ponytail. Mostly I was thinking about Sierra. Did she make it through the night? Would she ever recover? I decided not to think about that as I made my way slowly down the stairs. All my muscles had tied themselves into knots, and on top of the knots were bruises.

"How are you doing, honey?" my mom asked as I went into the kitchen.

As usual, my mom was already up. She was working on her variation of French toast. My mother refused to use white bread or any bleached flour products. She also had a thing against sugar. So when we had French toast it was made of whole-grain bread, and instead of syrup, we got honey. Don't ask me what made honey preferable to syrup. But for some reason my mom was okay with honey. I guess it was because she harvested it herself. She had several beehives out by her garden.

"I'm in pain," I told her as I eased myself onto a stool at the breakfast bar.

"Take some of this pain medicine," she told me as she pushed two pills at me. "And then take these vitamins."

Oh yeah, my mom was also a vitamin freak. A real pill pusher. But I obliged her by taking all the pills, one by one, and washing them down with a tall glass of organic apple juice. It wasn't bad really. The first time I had the other kind of apple juice, the kind that's amber colored but perfectly clear, I couldn't believe that people actually drank that stuff. It tasted bland and boring to me.

"Do you think I should call the hospital?" I asked.

"I don't see why not."

"Do you think they'll tell me anything?"

"All you can do is try."

And so I tried. I decided to ask about Sierra first, since she was in the worst shape last night.

"Are you a member of the family?" the woman on the other end demanded.

"No, but I was involved in the wreck."

"We're only allowed to give out information to direct family members."

"But I just want to know how she's doing," I pleaded. "Like is she okay or conscious or what?" I really wanted to say, "Did she survive?" but couldn't force those words out of my mouth.

"All I can tell you is that she's still in ICU and listed as serious condition."

"Thanks." I hung up the phone without bothering to ask about Ryun. Not that I wasn't concerned about him, I was. But I wanted to be sure Sierra was alive.

My mom set a plate of French toast in front of me. "How are they?"

"The hospital won't tell you much if you're not a family member. All I know is that Sierra is still in ICU and in serious condition."

Mom sadly shook her head. "That's too bad."

I attempted to eat a few bites of the French toast, then dumped the rest down the garbage disposal when my mom wasn't looking. "I've got to go see them," I said suddenly. "Do you think I could use your van?"

"Well, I guess so. I don't really have any plans today, other than puttering around in the green-house."

"Thanks." Then I left before she had a chance to change her mind.

As I was driving to the hospital, I wished I'd taken time to change my clothes. Then even the fact that I would think that felt weird. I never used to care what I wore or how I looked. But there I was, the day after a serious accident, going to see my two best friends who were still in bad shape and I was worried I didn't put on any lip gloss?

"Get real!" I told myself as I pulled into the hospital parking lot. The pain pills must have been helping a bit because I no longer ached with each movement. But I was still moving much more slowly than usual. It took forever to get inside the hospital. I asked directions to ICU, then headed for the elevators. I noticed a uniformed policeman getting into an elevator. Nervous that he might be the one who wanted to talk to me about the wreck, I paused to get a drink at the drinking fountain and waited to take the next ride up.

Somehow I managed to slip past the round ICU counter in the center of this large area. All the ICU rooms were on the perimeters and had wide windows. I guess that's so the nurses' station could watch everyone at once. I casually walked around, as if I knew what I was doing, until I saw Sierra's sister.

Jack, as Jacqueline liked to be called, was standing next to a bed where I could now see what must be Sierra. Her beautiful auburn hair had been cut, no, *hacked,* off. But even worse than that was her face. It was pale and swollen and covered with hideous cuts and bruises, almost to the point where you couldn't recognize her. There were all kinds of tubes and wires going into her and machines all around the bed. She didn't even look human anymore.

I covered my mouth with my hand. I wanted to turn away, to run from there and never come back. But somehow I didn't. Instead I just stood by the window watching her. Her eyes were closed. She didn't move a muscle. It didn't look good.

"McKenzie?"

I turned at the sound of my name. "Mrs. Reynolds," I said quickly. "I—uh—I am so sorry about Sierra." I felt tears in my eyes.

Mrs. Reynolds came up to me, and I could smell her expensive perfume as she took my sweaty trembling hand into her cool smooth one. "I'm sorry too," she said. "This whole thing is all so horrible."

I nodded. "I can't believe it happened. It seems so unreal."

She released my hand and stepped back, adjusting the shoulder strap of her sleek designer bag, which of course matched her shoes. "I'm just glad that you and Ryun weren't badly hurt."

"But Sierra," I said with a sob. "How—how is she doing?"

"We won't know for a while."

"She's still unconscious?"

She nodded and glanced into the room, where Jack was still standing by the bed. Jack actually appeared to be talking, although Sierra was obviously unconscious.

"Jacqueline thinks if she talks to her sister long enough that she'll snap out of it." Mrs. Reynolds sighed. "The doctors aren't quite as hopeful."

"But it can't hurt to try," I offered.

"No, of course not. I'm willing to try anything to get her back." She reached into the pocket of her moss-colored suede jacket and pulled out a perfect white handkerchief, then dabbed her eyes.

I glanced over my shoulder as I heard voices at the nurses' station. "I don't think I'm supposed to be in here," I said quietly.

"Yes, only immediate family members are allowed in ICU."

"I guess I better go. I want to see how Ryun is doing too."

"Thanks for checking on her, McKenzie. Sierra is lucky to have such a thoughtful friend." She reached for the door to Sierra's room. "Tell Ryun hello for me."

I felt like a traitor as I slinked away from the ICU area. The words *"Sierra is lucky to have such a thoughtful friend"* echoed over and over through my mind as I walked back to the elevators.

I'm a horrible person, I told myself as I pushed the button to go down. *I'm the one who should be in ICU right now, beaten and bruised and hooked up with all those wires and tubes. I'm the one who should've been seriously hurt in the accident last night. This is all my fault and I know it. But what can I do about it now?*

It didn't take long to locate Ryun's room. He wasn't awake yet, but his sister, Joon, was there, sitting right beside him.

She smiled at me as I walked in. "You're Kenzie, Ryun's friend."

"Yes," I said, wondering if Joon knew about us. Thankfully we didn't have long to talk because Ryun finally opened his eyes.

"There he is!" I said and leaned over to touch his hand. There was no way I could give him a kiss with Joon watching. I had to pretend to be just a friend.

"Finally, sleepyhead," Joon said. "We thought you were going to sleep forever."

Ryun rubbed his eyes and then his knee.

"Does it hurt?" I asked, wincing for him.

"Not really," Ryun said. "Guess the painkillers keep it down to a dull roar."

"Can I see?" Joon asked and moved closer to look at the stitches. Her eyes filled with tears. She said quickly, "Everything is going to be okay, Ry."

After we talked about what the doctors had said about his knee—that he'd have to wait for the swelling to go down and then he could have surgery—Joon stepped out for a minute. "Mom's on her way," she said. "I promised to meet her downstairs since she doesn't know her way around here yet." She grinned. "Wouldn't want her to get lost."

As soon as Joon left, Ryun glanced over at the empty bed on the other side of the room. "My roommate's doing his rehab right now. Close the door and come sit by me."

"How's everything going?" I asked as I closed the door.

"I guess things could be worse."

I pulled up a chair beside him and sat down. "Yeah, we could all three be dead."

"According to the paramedic who stopped by

to check on me a little bit ago, we all should've been dead. Did you know that there's almost nothing left of the car?"

"It looked pretty bad last night," I said.

He nodded. "How are you doing?"

"Just bruised and sore. Not much to complain about . . . especially after seeing Sierra today."

His eyes grew wide. "You saw her?"

"Yeah. She looks bad, Ryun. I mean really, really bad."

"Was she conscious?"

"No." I swallowed and played with the edge of the blanket on his bed. "She's still in a coma."

"Do you think she'll come out of it?"

"I spoke to her mom and she said they won't know for a while. But she didn't seem real hopeful either. She said that Jack keeps talking to her like she's going to wake up any minute."

He nodded. "That sounds like her sister."

"I feel so bad." I looked up at Ryun now.

"Yeah, me too." He ran his hand through his hair and sighed. "But there's nothing we can do about it now, Kenzie."

I looked down again and mumbled, "I know . . . but we should tell someone, shouldn't we?"

"Tell them what?" Ryun asked.

"You know . . . that Sierra wasn't the one driving."

"Why? Originally she *was* driving. And she was driving very dangerously too. She was going even faster than me and pretty much out of control. She could've easily killed us all."

"Yeah, I know."

"And if she hadn't pulled that crazy stunt about jumping out of the car, none of this would've happened."

"Yeah, you're right."

He nodded. "Of course I'm right. And how fair would it be for us to pay the price for what Sierra was doing? Think about it, Kenzie. . . . What were you doing right before the wreck?"

"I was trying to hold on to Sierra, to keep her from jumping. I mean, she had the door open and—"

"That's right," he said. "And I was trying to help you hold on to her. It's Sierra's fault that we got in the wreck." He shook his head now. "She might as well have been driving."

Everything he said was true, so it was hard to argue. "But when Sierra wakes up . . ."

Ryun was silent for a minute, then said, "But what if she doesn't?"

I shuddered. "She has to wake up."

"I hope so too. And when she does, we'll deal with it then."

"Wouldn't it be easier if we just tell the truth now?"

"Kenzie," he said, "we're not lying. We're just not telling everything. We may not have to . . ."

"It's my fault," I said, and my voice cracked.

"No, it's not," he told me firmly. "You weren't driving."

"But she called me her best friend, and I . . ."

"We," Ryun shot back. "It wasn't just you who got her upset. We both did. And *I* was the one driving."

"I know, but . . ."

"It'll be okay, Kenzie," he said softly.

He squeezed my hand and pulled me toward him now. "We need to hang together on this, Kenzie."

I leaned in and stared into his handsome face, getting lost in his eyes. "I guess it can't really hurt anything," I said quietly. "I mean, it's not like Sierra's going to get into any trouble or anything. . . ."

"Exactly." He pulled me closer and we kissed.

"It's not as if she'd been drinking or had her license revoked or anything. . . ."

He ran his finger down my cheek. "It makes perfect sense."

I nodded. "I just wish she'd get better."

"So do I," he assured me and we kissed again.

Then we heard the door opening, so I scooted back into my chair as Joon and her mom walked in with a box of chocolate-covered cherries.

"My favorite," Ryun said as he tore open the box. "Want one, Kenzie?"

"No, I think I should get going."

Joon stepped up and looked at me more closely now. "You were in the wreck too?"

I nodded.

"Wow, looks like you fared pretty well."

"Just lucky, I guess."

"I'll say."

"See you, Ryun," I called as I headed for the door.

"Thanks for filling me in on Sierra," he said, probably for his sister's benefit.

"How *is* Sierra?" I heard her asking him as I stepped out into the hall.

But I hurried away. I didn't want to hear his

answer, didn't want to see him continuing the game we'd been playing for too long already. I was tired of all the sneaking around, the deceit, the betrayal. I wanted the game to be over. But it seemed we'd just begun.

16

kenzie's story

As I left Ryun's room, I heard someone calling my name. I turned and saw a uniformed officer hurrying down the hall toward me. He looked familiar, and then I realized that he was at the scene of the accident last night. Was it just last night? It seemed like another lifetime ago.

"McKenzie?"

I nodded without answering.

"Good, I thought that was you. Do you remember me?"

"Sort of."

He stuck out his hand. "I'm Officer Williams."

"Right."

"So, how are you feeling today?"

"Like I got hit by a truck."

"That sounds about right." He smiled. He seemed

137

a little young for a cop and was surprisingly good-looking too. "You got a few minutes to talk?"

"I—uh—I guess so."

"Want to get a soda or a cup of coffee?" he offered as he led me toward the elevators.

We ended up in the cafeteria at a table off to one side and next to a large picture window. I pretended to be very focused on doctoring up my coffee with just the right amount of cream and sugar, then stir-stir-stir. I was afraid to look up into his face.

He made small talk for a bit, commenting on Highview High's football team and how he still remembered his senior year. Then he actually talked about the weather before finally cutting to the chase. "I need to get your account of the accident, McKenzie." He took out a little black notebook, flipped it open, and with pen poised, waited for me to begin.

"What do you mean?" I asked.

"It's no big deal, really," he assured me. "We just need your account for our records. Can you tell me in your own words exactly what happened last night? As you remember it." When he smiled again, I thought, *He should become a poster boy for recruiting cops.*

"Okay," I said slowly. "But where do I begin?"

"Let's start with where you kids were shortly before the wreck. Where were you driving from?"

"We went to the game," I began.

Officer Williams nodded eagerly, as if I'd said something brilliant.

"Sierra had invited me to ride with her to the game. And then we picked up Ryun."

"So Sierra was driving?"

"Yeah," I said. "She'd gotten her dad's car for the night. It was a '57 Chevy, but I guess you know that already."

"That's okay. Just tell me what happened like I don't know anything."

"Right. Anyway, we left the game and got into her car—and she was kind of excited, you know."

"Had she had anything to drink?"

"You mean alcohol?"

He nodded.

"No, well, not that I know of."

"Does she ever drink?"

I decided that honesty would be the best policy. Everyone knew that Sierra drank a beer or two once in a while. Most of the kids in her crowd drank occasionally. "Yeah, sometimes."

"But she hadn't had anything last night?"

"I don't think so."

"Had she used anything else that might've impaired her driving in any way?"

"You mean like drugs?"

"Yeah, drugs, grass, diet pills, whatever."

"No, nothing like that. Sierra isn't into drugs."

He continued writing. "So you three were going down Route 58?"

"Yeah. And like I said she was kind of excited."

"She was driving fast?"

"Well, not speeding, I guess. But it just seemed like everything was happening really fast, you know?"

"I suppose it does seem like that, looking back."

"Yeah, maybe that's it. Anyway, we were suddenly veering off the road, toward the right, and I could tell we were in the gravel on the shoulder. I think maybe I screamed then." I paused to think about my words. "I can't really remember exactly. All I know is that we were back on the road, only going sort of sideways and over the middle line and clear off the road again on the left side, and then the car flipped and we rolled a few times." I shook my head. "It was really crazy."

"Did you have on seat belts?"

"No. I'm not even sure if the car had them or not."

He nodded and continued to write. "So the car stops rolling . . ."

"Yeah. It landed upside down, and we were just sort of all over the place in it. I don't even totally remember how I got out of it, but I do remember that when I called for Sierra she didn't answer. That's when Ryun and I realized she was still inside the car. We pulled Sierra out of the car and dragged her away from it just as the whole thing went up in flames."

He nodded. "What happened then?"

"I just remember staying with Sierra. It wasn't long before the ambulance came. I don't even know how they found out about us."

"Another car stopped when they saw the wreck and called 911 on their cell phone."

"We would've called too, but Sierra's cell phone was in her purse, and her purse was still in the car.

And Ryun's must have fallen out of his pocket when he crawled out."

"You guys had quite a night."

"It just seems so unreal," I said. "I keep thinking it's only a bad dream and that I'll wake up soon and everything will be okay—and that Sierra will be just fine—" Suddenly I was crying again. Officer Williams handed me a paper napkin to wipe my eyes with, and I apologized to him for being so emotional.

"Hey, it's okay. You've been through quite an ordeal."

"I guess . . . although it doesn't seem like much compared to what Sierra's gone through—or is going through."

"Yeah, it doesn't look too good for her."

"What do you mean?" I asked. "Did you hear something new?"

"Probably the same thing you've already heard." He looked out the window now, as if he really didn't want to discuss it.

"You mean that she might not recover?"

He nodded sadly. "She had so much going for her too."

I began to feel sick to my stomach. I wasn't sure if it was from the coffee or the conversation. "Is that all?" I asked as I reached for my bag.

"I guess so. That is, unless you think of anything you may have left out."

"I'd better go. I'm borrowing my mom's van, and she needs it back soon."

"Drive carefully," he warned me, and I hurried from the cafeteria as if I had some place important to go. I resisted the urge to run back up to Ryun's room and pour out my story, telling him everything that just happened and how awful it was making me feel. But I was worried that Officer Williams might see me and get suspicious. My palms were clammy and I felt jittery as I climbed into the van. I knew I'd never be able to pass a lie-detector test, so I hoped the police never had to question me again. I reminded myself that I hadn't actually *lied* to Officer Williams. I just left some important things out.

By the time I got home, every bone in my body was aching and throbbing. I found my mom in the kitchen scrubbing potatoes and handed her the van keys.

"Are you okay, honey?" she asked, pausing from her chore to really look at me.

"I don't feel so good."

She put down a potato and placed her cool damp hand on my forehead. "What hurts exactly?"

"Everything," I told her. "I just ache all over."

"Well, it's been almost four hours since you took any pills. Why don't you take a couple more, then go have a nice hot bath and then take a nap?"

I trudged upstairs and followed her orders.

When I woke up from my nap it was almost three o'clock. Lark was standing in my doorway with the cordless phone in her hand.

"It's for you," she said as she brought it over to me. "Feeling better?"

I nodded and took the phone. "Hello?"

"Finally," said an exasperated voice.

"Holly?"

"Yes. We heard the news, Kenzie. Didn't your mom tell you that I'd been calling?"

"I was at the hospital this morning. Then I went back to bed after I got home. Sorry."

"No, I'm sorry. How are you feeling?"

"Pretty crappy."

"But at least you're not in the hospital."

"No."

"Have you heard how Sierra and Ryun are doing?"

"Sierra was still in a coma this morning. Ryun's knee is pretty messed up."

"Yeah, I just talked to Ryun. Man, Kenzie, this is all so unbelievable."

"Tell me about it."

"What happened last night?"

I briefly recounted the wreck story to her, telling it the same way I told Officer Williams this morning. I figured it was probably good practice.

"So she knew about you and Ryun?"

I hadn't exactly told Holly that, but then she'd been in on the whole thing last night.

"Yeah, she knew," I admitted.

"Did you tell her?"

"No, she heard us talking, Holly, in the bathroom during halftime."

"Sierra was in the bathroom?"

"Apparently."

"Oh no."

"Oh yes."

"And that's why she was driving so crazy?"

"She was pretty upset, Holly."

"Wow."

I sighed and leaned back onto my pillow, closing my eyes and wishing that this would all just go away. "Please don't tell anyone, Holly. We don't want everyone thinking that Sierra was driving crazy. The police are already questioning whether or not she'd been drinking."

"Had she?"

"No, of course not."

"Well, it's not like she's going to get into trouble for getting into a wreck."

"No, but it'll only make it harder on her parents if they find out that she was driving recklessly last night."

"Yeah, I guess you're right. . . . Do you think she's going to make it, Kenzie?"

"I—uh—I don't know."

"My mom said that the church prayer chain called this morning and asked her to pray for Sierra. She said it didn't sound good."

"Yeah. My mom was the one who called it in to start with," I said.

"Well, I'm not much into prayers, but I'm praying for her."

"Yeah, me too." But the truth was, I hadn't been praying. I was too afraid that God wouldn't want to listen to me. After all, I hadn't spoken to him much lately, so what right did I have to come crying to him now?

"Are you going back over to the hospital again today?"

I considered this. "I'd like to."

"Do you want a ride?"

"Were you going over?"

"If you need a ride, I am."

"Thanks, Holly, I'd really appreciate it."

So we arranged to go over during the evening visiting hours. I told her that we wouldn't be able to see Sierra in ICU, but we could check on Ryun. Then I called Ryun to make sure he was up for company.

"Sure," he said in a glum voice. "I could use some distraction."

"Distraction?"

"Yeah, whatever."

"What is it?" I asked.

"I got the results on my knee injury."

"Is it bad?"

"It's not good."

"But can they fix it?"

"Yeah, that's the plan."

"I'll bet you're going to be just fine, Ryun." I tried to sound positive, the way I know Sierra would sound if she were talking to him right now. "You know how great medical technology is. They can fix almost anything."

"Yeah." His voice brightened. "Let's hope so."

Then I told him about my conversation with Officer Williams.

"He came by here too."

"Did you tell him the same thing?" Suddenly I was worried. What if Ryun had changed his mind at the last minute? What if he had decided to tell the truth—the whole truth and nothing but the truth? What kind of trouble would I be in?

"Yeah."

I sighed in relief.

"We can talk more later," he said quietly. "My sister's still here."

"That's nice. Tell her hi for me."

"I will."

"And I'll see you around seven."

I felt a tiny bit better after I hung up. Maybe Ryun was right about the whole thing with the police. That what they didn't know wouldn't hurt them—or us. And maybe it was the best route for everyone, including Sierra. Either way it was too late to turn back now.

17

Several days after the accident, Sierra
was moved from ICU to a room downstairs where
she could have visitors. Not that she knew anyone
was there since she was still fast asleep. She
reminded me of Sleeping Beauty, only her face
was so messed up that you could barely recognize
her. It was probably good she was still in a coma—
although I really did want her to wake up . . . someday. But if she were conscious right now and saw
her face, well, knowing Sierra, I felt sure she'd want
to die.

I walked by her room and peered in every time
I came to the hospital, which had been every single
day since the accident. I saw Jack talking to Sierra
as if Sierra could really hear her. Jack insisted that
Sierra could hear everything. She got mad if anyone
said anything negative. It was sweet, really, but

unnerving. Especially considering all that happened the night of the wreck.

All three of us made the front page of the Sunday paper. Photos and everything. They wrote it up as if Ryun and I were the biggest heroes for rescuing Sierra from the burning car. Kind of sickening, really. Mom wanted me to save the article, but I told her I didn't want to be reminded of the worst night of my life. So she said she'd keep it for me—that someday I would appreciate it.

■　■　■

Ryun was released from the hospital on Tuesday but probably wouldn't be back in school until next week. I didn't blame him for putting it off as long as possible. I finally went in today, Wednesday, and it was almost more than I could stand with everyone acting like I was such a hero for rescuing Sierra that night.

"How're you doing?" Holly asked me just before lunch.

"I'm getting out of here," I told her as I got some things from my locker.

"You don't want to stick around for lunch and see if you can get some more pats on the back?"

I scowled at her.

"Sorry." She smiled, then glanced over her shoulder to see if anyone was listening. Then she lowered her voice. "Just the same, you should be happy to know that nobody seems to know anything about you and Ryun."

"Really? Carin came by to see Ryun, so I guess that's good then," I said. I acted like that was a huge relief, although I wasn't all that thrilled to hear that Ryun told Carin he still loved Sierra.

"So, lighten up, Kenzie. It's not the end of the world, you know."

"Maybe not for me. But I still feel terrible about Sierra."

She nodded. "We all do. But you can't beat yourself up forever. It's not like you were the one behind the wheel that night."

Well, that was true enough. But I might as well have been.

I went back to work at Little Lambs today, and it was the best medicine so far. I could forget myself and my problems when I was with these kids. The five hours flew by. It wasn't until the way home that I remembered how messed up my life was.

"Phone for you," Lark informed me as soon as I was in the door. "A guy."

Suspecting it was Ryun I took the phone up to my room and closed the door. "Hello?"

"Kenzie, I miss you."

In spite of the day I'd had at school, I smiled. "I miss you too, Ryun."

"How was it at school?"

"Pretty weird."

"What happened?"

"We're the hometown heroes," I told him sarcastically.

"That's okay," he said. "We did save her life."

"Yeah, I guess."

"We *did,* Kenzie. If we hadn't dragged her out, she'd be dead."

"Well, she's not much better than dead now."

He didn't respond, and I felt bad. "Sorry," I said. "I'm just feeling bummed."

"We've got to move on, Kenzie."

"Yeah, that's what Holly was saying today. I'm just not sure how you do that."

"Just give it some time, Kenzie. Things will get better."

"I hope you're right." I swallowed hard, afraid I was about to start crying again. "I don't think I'll be able to go on like this for too much longer. . . . I hear you convinced Carin that you and Sierra are still madly in love."

"I'm sorry, Kenzie." I heard him exhale loudly. "But you've got to understand that I had to do that. How would it sound if I told everyone that we'd broken up right before the wreck?"

"I know. I know."

"Trust me with this, okay, Kenzie? Really, it's going to get better in time."

And so that was what I kept telling myself. *It will get better in time.* I must have told myself that about 50 times a day. It became my mantra. The only problem was, I was afraid it wasn't true. I had two major fears. The first was that Sierra was going to wake up and tell the world that Ryun and I were liars and cheats. And the second? That she wouldn't wake up at all. Either way, I didn't see how it could ever get better.

Sometimes I actually wondered if I could be

making myself mentally ill with all the stress. Maybe one morning I'd wake up, blathering away like a complete idiot. But maybe by then it wouldn't matter.

More and more, I felt like I was walking through a foggy haze. I went to my morning classes and tried to pay attention, take notes, and act normal. I smiled around my friends and sometimes even laughed, although it made me feel guilty inside. It seemed wrong to laugh when Sierra was stuck in that hospital bed, still unconscious.

Then I usually skipped lunch since it was too hard to act normal that long. Instead I went straight to my job at Little Lambs—the only part of my day that felt real. If anything had the potential to help me get out of this fog, it would be the kids at Little Lambs. Their hugs don't have strings attached. Sometimes I wished I could shrink myself down to their size and their age—and just start all over again.

Ryun and I agreed not to be seen together in public, at least for now. The only exception was when we visited Sierra in the hospital. My excuse was that I didn't have a car, and my other ride opportunities, like Holly and Carin, were often busy with cheerleading practice and related stuff. But I always looked forward to that time alone with Ryun. It was the only thing that made all this pain a little worthwhile.

A week passed, and I discovered that Ryun may have been right after all. I really did begin to feel better. And, amazingly, I slowly adjusted to Sierra's unchanging condition and accepted the possibility that she might never recover. Of course, I still felt guilty. But there wasn't much I could do about it.

As Sierra's 18th birthday approached, I organized an impromptu birthday party in Sierra's hospital room. She probably had no idea we were there, but it was the least I could do. I got a cake and balloons and the works. And although Sierra didn't even flutter an eyelid, we girls laughed and talked and finally sang a rousing chorus of "Happy Birthday."

Then it was over and everything was cleaned up. I just stood there in front of Sierra's bed, staring at her still bruised and disfigured face and her badly cropped hair. I felt so hopeless. "Happy Birthday, Sierra," I muttered, then left the room.

Just when I accepted that Sierra was probably never going to come out of the coma, Ryun called me and said she woke up.

"What?" I gasped. I closed my bedroom door and collapsed on the bed, my heart pounding in my ears.

"Sierra is awake." He said the words slowly and deliberately, as if he was also just absorbing this fact.

"Are you serious?" I felt my world spinning out of control again. I imagined Sierra sitting up in bed and telling everyone—the police, the newspaper, all our friends and family—*the truth*. And the truth was going to hurt.

"I wouldn't joke about something like this." His voice sounded strange to me, low and flat.

"Have you—have you seen her yet, Ryun?" I was afraid to hear his answer.

"No. I just heard about it. Her sister called me a few minutes ago—to tell me the good news."

"What did Jack say? I mean, is Sierra talking? Is she normal? Does she remember what—?"

"Jacqueline didn't give me specifics. She just said that Sierra's awake and she thought I'd want to know."

"What are we going to do?"

Long pause. "I'm not sure."

"We should go see her." Yet even as I said these words I wondered why.

"I know."

I glanced at the clock. It wasn't quite 7:00 yet. "It's still visiting hours."

"I know."

"Ryun?"

"Yeah?"

"Are you okay?"

"I—uh—well, you know. It's just going to be hard. I mean, what do we say? How do we act?"

I could tell that Ryun was just as shaken as I was, maybe even more. I decided it was time for me to be the strong one for a change. "We just go in there and we act perfectly normal. And whatever happens . . . happens."

"Right."

"What else can we do?"

"Run?" Then he kind of laughed so I'd know he wasn't really serious. But I had to admit—the idea of running away did have a certain appeal. Especially if I was running away with Ryun.

"Yeah, maybe we could head on down to Mexico." I forced a lightness I didn't feel into my voice.

He exhaled loudly. "I'll pick you up in about 15 minutes."

"Okay." I hung up and immediately began pacing back and forth in my room, wondering what would happen now. Would Ryun and I be in trouble with the police? Would it be better just to confess everything immediately, to admit we were scared, that things got out of control? Could I claim temporary insanity or short-term amnesia? I wondered how my parents would react. Would they be disappointed in me, never trust me again? Or would they practice what they preached and forgive me and move on? I thought they'd forgive me, but I knew it was going to be humiliating for a while.

As I brushed my hair I actually found myself praying, which just showed how terrified I really was. Suddenly the stakes were higher than ever and I found myself trying to make a deal with God.

"If you will just straighten this mess out," I pleaded, "I promise I'll live differently from now on. I'll go to church more, and I'll read my Bible and pray. Just, please, I beg you, straighten this out."

Then, taking a deep breath, I prepared myself to tell my parents the latest news and started down the stairs.

Everyone was in the family room. Lark was on the computer that Dad insisted we keep out in the open so there was no "hanky-panky" going on. And Mom was helping the twins with their homework—it looked like math tonight. Dad was flopped

out in his old blue recliner reading one of his contractor magazines. He was still wearing his dusty
jeans and plaid flannel shirt, and my mom still had
on her apron, the one with the big red apple on the
front. The twins, in the midst of a little argument,
could have both used a haircut.

The theme of our family room was farm animals.
Don't ask me why. Maybe it was because it was next
to the kitchen and Mom thought horses, cows, and
pigs would go nicely with apples. But as I looked
at the five of them in there, I imagined that they
were a farm family, just relaxing after a hard day's
work in the fields.

"Is that you, honey?" My mom looked up from
the math book.

"Yeah." I stepped from the shadows into the
family room. "I wanted to tell you guys the good
news."

"What's that?" My dad put his magazine down.

"Sierra is conscious."

"Praise God!" my mom exclaimed. "That's the
most wonderful news. How's she doing?"

"I—uh—I don't know. Ryun is picking me up and
we're going over to see her now. If you don't mind."

"Of course not," said Mom. "And be sure to give
her our love."

"Okay."

And then, a few minutes later, Ryun and I were
heading toward the hospital. But unlike the other
trips when I actually enjoyed his company, all I
could think of was that we were both going to be
in serious trouble before the night was over.

"Maybe we should just get everything out into the open," I told him. "Just admit to Sierra that we got scared and lied. She might even understand, Ryun, especially if she thought it was to protect you. She may still have feelings for you. And you could pretend that you still love her, and I can act like what happened between us was nothing, just a onetime slip up that I totally regret." I heard myself talking fast, possibly making no sense, but I was desperate. I wanted to get out of this mess as smoothly and quickly as possible. "It wouldn't even matter if she was so mad at me that we couldn't be friends anymore. I deserve as much."

"Take a deep breath," said Ryun. "You're getting way too stressed about this."

"And you're not?"

"We don't know how she's going to react. Let's just play it by ear," he said calmly.

I did take a deep breath. But as Ryun parked his Explorer, I knew we were only minutes away from what could turn very ugly. Just as we stepped into the elevator I fell apart. "I can't do this, Ryun. I'm sorry, but it's too hard." I began to sob. "I just need to go home. I'm sorry—"

He took me in his arms and held me, whispering into my ear, "It's going to be all right, Kenzie. Really. Just trust me. Whatever happens, you and I will stick together. Even if everyone else turns against us, we still have each other. *Right?*"

I looked into his eyes and finally nodded. "Right." Then I braced myself, trying to believe I could do this. "Sorry," I told him as we proceeded down the hall toward her room. "I'll try to keep it together."

And, amazingly, I did. I started chattering at Sierra as soon as we entered the room. I knew it was raw nerves doing the talking, but I thought, *If I can just keep this light conversation going long enough—if we can just get past the initial awkwardness—then everything might be okay.*

Incredibly, it worked. Sierra responded positively to my unending stream of words. I told her how everyone at school was doing, going into way too much detail and description over stupid things like clothes and shoes, but she listened intently and even asked questions at times.

I tried not to stare at her face as I blabbered on and on about basically nothing. Her bruises and scars appeared worse now that she was awake and conscious. Before she had just looked broken and lifeless, like she wasn't even real. But now with her eyes open and expressions registering on her face, she looked hideous. I was scared that if I looked too long, I would totally lose it again and start crying. So the nonstop talking was a safety zone for me.

Her gaze darted back and forth from me to Ryun, mostly keeping her eyes upon him, and I wondered what she was really thinking. But instead of giving her a chance to voice her thoughts or ask questions, I just kept talking. Like I was in a talkathon and was almost unaware of what I was really saying.

But Ryun seemed to be relaxing now that I'd relieved the pressure. So when I needed to pause and literally catch my breath, he stepped in and took over for me.

When Sierra called Ryun over to her bedside, she noticed that he was limping. And she felt really bad because she assumed his injury was her fault. I had to turn away just then, because I was sure I'd start crying and spill the beans and completely ruin Ryun's future.

I watched as the two of them began to talk. But I could tell by Sierra's eyes that she definitely still had feelings for him, and I wasn't convinced he didn't still have feelings for her. He held her hand and told her how worried he'd been, how glad he was that she was recovering.

I knew it was all an act—a clever way to make Sierra forgive us for making such a complete mess of things. So I tried not to feel jealous. I reminded myself that I deserved to feel bad. It was a small price to pay to move past all this.

Then I realized that she was beginning to talk about that night—and I froze, thinking, *Here it comes.* But she said she didn't have any memory of the accident. She could remember going to the game and driving her dad's car, but that was where it all ended. She had amnesia.

Maybe this is God's way of getting us out of this mess, I thought. The only thing I knew about amnesia was that it wasn't permanent—but TV shows conveniently used it to make a plot work. But what about in real life? I wondered. Maybe Sierra's amnesia might buy us some valuable time. Maybe Ryun would get a chance to reestablish her trust and she would see that we weren't the horrible friends she thought we were that night. It might be a fresh start for everyone. . . .

Or she might remember and be absolutely furious at us for all that we did before the wreck, as well as for not being honest with her now. Again I considered just confessing everything and taking whatever consequences came my way. But then what would happen to Ryun?

At last we were back in Ryun's Explorer. "I think it's going to be okay," he said as he pulled out of the parking lot.

"Really?" I wasn't so sure.

"Yeah. I think it's all going to work out."

"But what if her memory comes back?"

"We'll do like you said earlier, Kenzie."

"Huh?" I'd said so many things earlier—like diarrhea of the mouth—that I had no idea what he was talking about.

"We'll tell her we're really sorry and that we were scared at the time and just did what we had to in order to get by. In the meantime I'll just keep playing the loyal boyfriend and maybe she'll be able to put it all behind her."

"You think so?"

He shrugged. "Time will tell."

I leaned back into the seat and sighed. "It was kind of a relief though, wasn't it?"

"That she's lost her memory?"

"Yeah."

"What a stroke of luck."

But was it? I wondered.

Ryun and I continued visiting Sierra. It got easier each time we went in. I began to relax and think that maybe, just maybe, we would make it through this thing after all.

Still it bothered me a lot that we had to keep up the charade so we wouldn't look totally uncaring. I played the loyal best friend, doing everything I could to make sure that her recovery was as smooth as possible. Ryun, of course, played the devoted boyfriend who loved Sierra even if her face did look like something out of a horror flick. We should have gotten Oscars.

It wasn't that I didn't like Sierra. I really did.

And it wasn't that I wasn't totally thankful she was recovering. I really was.

I guess I was just worried that I might somehow

mess up and blow our cover and ruin everything. I was walking a tightrope—a never-ending tightrope—and I was scared that one of these days I'd miss my step and that would be it.

"You seem different," Anna told me during art class today. We'd actually started sitting together again. I guess it was a result of the wreck and her unexpected sympathy toward me. In some ways, I found her company soothing. I didn't have to perform for her. At least not like I had to with friends like Holly or Carin and, most of all, Sierra. Still, I had to keep up my guard. There were certain secrets I could share with no one except Ryun. I didn't know what I would do without him.

"Different, how?" I asked as I attempted a half-hearted charcoal sketch of a sculpture our teacher had placed on the front table. We were working on shadows and light.

"Kind of stressed and unhappy."

I nodded as I tried to create a realistic shadow. "Well, life's been hard, you know."

"Maybe . . . but it seems like it should be getting a lot easier now that Sierra is getting better."

I sighed. "I guess I'm just a little worn out." That was true. "I mean, I go to school, then I go to work, then I go to visit Sierra some days. Then I go home and do homework . . . and the next day I do it all again."

"You're a good friend to Sierra," Anna said, like she meant it.

She said it nicely, but I felt the stab in her observation. I hadn't proved myself to be that loyal of a friend to anyone. Not to Anna. Not to Sierra. The only one I'd really been loyal to was Ryun. I'd laid it all on the line for Ryun. But then that was different.

I decided to try going to church on Sundays again, which pleased my parents. And it really wasn't so bad, although I usually left the service feeling torn. How could I go on living a lie? Then I would spend the afternoon—and the rest of the week—trying to convince myself that I was just doing what needed to be done to make it through this thing called life. I could rationalize it all and move on, until Sunday came around again.

However, Wednesdays were still mine. I didn't go to the midweek service or youth group. And Ryun and I still tried to meet on those nights, at least when it worked or when we weren't going over to the hospital to see Sierra.

Ryun finally got his call from Duke offering him the scholarship he'd been dreaming of. Naturally, he accepted. But I was surprised when he said he didn't tell the coach about his knee injury.

"I can do this," he assured me as we drove to the hospital to visit Sierra. "I'll have my surgery this week, and after that I'll do my therapy. I'll be ready to play by the beginning of summer and by fall I'll be as good as new."

"Really?"

"Sure." His smile convinced me he knew what he was talking about.

That night Sierra's face was looking much more normal, plus her hair had been cut into a cute style, by her mom of all people. Who knew? But as I watched her and Ryun holding hands and laughing as they looked into each others' eyes, I had to excuse myself from the room. I went down to the cafeteria and made myself a cup of herbal tea. *Just chill. Calm down. Get over it. It's all just part of the game,* I told myself.

But I wasn't so sure anymore. Was I the one being taken for a ride? Could Ryun be leading me on just to keep me under his thumb and going along with his story? The very thought scared me—a lot.

Then Ryun showed up and apologized. "I know that must make you feel lousy, Kenzie." He ran his hand through his hair. "And, believe me, it makes me feel terrible too. But we've got to play along for a while longer. At least until she gets out of the hospital. After that I'll figure out a way to break up with her."

"Really?" I felt hope reviving. "How long do you think?"

"She could be released from the hospital by Christmas."

"You can't break up with her at Christmas." I couldn't believe I was saying this.

"No, you're right. It'll have to be after she's been back at school for a while. After the newness of her being back wears off."

"And the sympathy factor dies down a little?"

He nodded. "Yeah, that would make it a lot easier for both of us."

And so I consoled myself with the promise that we would be together sometime in the new year. I could wait that long, right?

But then everything started to change. Not in a big way, but I could feel something was different during our next visits. I was becoming more and more uncomfortable around Sierra. Maybe it was paranoid, but I got the feeling she knew something . . . or that her memory was kicking in. She hadn't said anything, but sometimes I saw this look in her eye—like she hated my guts and wished I were dead. I nudged Ryun and tried to signal him that something wasn't right, but he didn't seem to get it. He just smiled at me like everything was cool. So I tugged on his arm.

"We should go," I said, even though we'd been there only a few minutes. So Ryun leaned over and kissed Sierra on the forehead. He told her he had homework and we left. My heart was pounding in my chest as we walked to the elevator.

"What gives?" he asked as he punched the buttons.

I steadied myself. *"She knows."*

His eyes got big. "What do you mean?"

"I can just feel it, Ryun. She's remembering something. I could see it in her eyes."

He put his arm around my shoulders. "You're just getting yourself worked up, Kenzie. You're imagining things." He stroked my hair and I began to calm down.

But after tonight, I no longer wanted to visit Sierra. "I don't want to go to the hospital tomorrow," I told Ryun when he stopped in front of my house. "You can go if you want, but I can't take it."

"But she'll ask about—"

"Just tell her I have too much homework or

something," I said as I reached for the door handle. "Besides," I teased him, "she'll probably be glad to have you all to herself."

Then he pulled me toward him, kissing me and promising that it wouldn't be long before our little game came to an end.

Ryun returned to the hospital for his knee surgery on the Thursday before winter break. I told my parents to pray for him before I went to school that morning. Then I convinced my mom to let me leave Little Lambs an hour early just so I could check on him. It was all I could think about all day long. How would it go? Would he be able to play soccer again?

20

Right after work, I headed toward the hospital to see Ryun. Even though I hadn't been able to pray for myself, I'd prayed off and on all day for Ryun.

When I burst into his room, his sister, Joon, was there. She looked up at me with mild curiosity but didn't move from her post next to his bed. I could tell she was feeling territorial toward her brother, and I didn't blame her. In fact, it was kind of sweet. I could imagine Lark doing that for me if I were in this position.

"How is he?" I whispered to Joon since it seemed that Ryun was sleeping.

"He's just fine," Ryun answered in a groggy voice.

I laughed. "Sorry to wake you."

"Come on over here," he said sleepily. "So I can see you better."

So I walked around to the other side of the bed and peered into his glazed eyes. "Enjoying those pain meds?" I asked him.

He tossed me a goofy grin as he took my hand. I was a little surprised by this public display of affection in front of his little sister. But then we could always blame it on the meds.

"The surgery seemed to go well," Joon offered as she stood up on the other side of the bed, looking down at her brother.

"That's good to hear, Joon." I smiled at her. "Does it look like he'll be hitting the soccer field anytime soon?"

She nodded. "After he recovers and goes through a bunch of therapy. But he should be ready to play by summer."

"By summer? Wow, that sounds really great."

Ryun chuckled. "Yeah, Joon has it all figured out." He reached over and grabbed her hand with his free one. "Ryun Lee will be starting for Duke next year—as good as new."

I reluctantly let go of Ryun's hand. "I should probably go say hi to Sierra." But the truth was, I'd rather *not* see her. Just the same, I knew it would look bad if anyone saw me visiting Ryun and not her.

"Tell her hey for me," he said.

"Okay," I told him. "You take care now. See you, Joon."

Then I walked over to Sierra's room, my heels

dragging with each step. But when I stepped into her room, she was asleep. I was so relieved that I actually smiled. That was when I noticed the ancient old woman—was her name Mississippi or Missouri?—in the next bed. She seemed to be studying me carefully. I smiled and waved at her, then tiptoed away.

I visited Ryun as much as I could the next couple of days. And I went to Sierra's room too. But when I saw her family there I just smiled and waved and told her I'd come back later. I didn't. I figured lots of our other friends would be visiting her, or so I told myself, since it was Christmas break now.

I didn't see Sierra for a whole week. And I only decided to go then because the guilt was eating me alive, plus Ryun insisted that I needed to go see her before she started getting suspicious.

"I thought she was going to be released by now," I told him. I knew I sounded petty, like I was complaining that Sierra was inconveniencing me by still being in the hospital. And it wasn't what I meant, exactly. But then I wasn't even sure what I meant.

On Christmas Eve Ryun stopped by my house after visiting Sierra at the hospital. We stood outside on my porch (for privacy's sake), bundled up in our winter coats and sipping homemade hot chocolate with real whipped cream. Naturally, these were generously provided by my mom, who was using that as an excuse to check up on us. "Don't you guys want to come in out of the cold?" she asked innocently. But we assured her that we were perfectly fine and waited for her to go back inside.

"I thought Sierra would be home by now too,"

Ryun said. "But I guess it was easier to keep up with her therapy in the hospital."

"Too bad." I blew the steam off the top of my cup.

"Can you imagine how depressing it would be to spend Christmas in there?" he said. "Don't you think you should at least drop by and say merry Christmas?"

"Isn't it enough that I helped you pick out a Christmas present for her?"

"And you were right about it. She liked the book very much. Thank you."

Then, making sure that my mom—or more likely Lark—wasn't peeking out the window at us, I let Ryun kiss me before he went back home to celebrate Christmas with his own family.

"Be careful on the ice," I called out as I watched him limping to his car.

■   ■   ■

I waited until the afternoon of the next day, Christmas Day, to gather a few friends (for moral support) before I called Sierra and asked if it was a good time to visit. I was halfway hoping that she'd have family there and not want additional visitors. But she said, "Come on over."

I felt uncomfortable as we rode over in Holly's Jeep. It was just Carin and Holly and me. "Have you guys been in to see her much?" I asked as we were riding the elevator up.

"I came early on," admitted Holly. "But I haven't been since she regained consciousness."

"Really?" I'd always thought they were closer than that.

"I'm not very good in hospitals," Carin said. "I hear her face is pretty awful. . . ."

"Yeah," Holly agreed. "It was pretty nasty."

"Well, she looks okay now," I assured them as we approached her room. Then we stood outside her door for a few seconds as Holly and Carin got cold feet.

"You go first," said Holly as she gave me a shove into the room.

Surprised, I practically fell on my face as I stumbled in. It was the first time I'd worn these new boots that Holly talked me into buying last fall and I was still getting used to the heels. "Merry Christmas," I said as I attempted to regain my composure.

I remembered the T-shirt that I'd picked out with Ryun not long ago. We were getting a quick cup of coffee at one of those little strip malls where we knew no one would be around to recognize us. "Should I get this for Sierra's Christmas present?" I'd asked half joking, and he'd just shrugged and said, "Why not?" Now I wasn't so sure.

Just the same I removed the navy T-shirt from my purse and laid it out on her bed, suddenly wishing I hadn't brought it. On the front were tiny white letters that spelled *If you can read this, BACK OFF! You're too close.*

"You know, for when you go back to school," I explained. "So nobody bumps you in the halls?"

"Thanks, Kenzie. You are *such* a great friend."

I heard the fake sweetness just dripping from her voice.

Carin was still standing out in the hallway, but Holly came in and began to chatter nervously. In fact, she reminded me of me the first time I saw Sierra after she came out of the coma. Finally Carin stepped in with a bag of magazines. I tried to remain calm, act natural. I told myself that everything would be okay.

And then Sierra dropped a real bombshell by telling everyone that she and Ryun spent Christmas Eve together last night. I suddenly wondered— did he lie to me about going home to be with his family? Had he really come back here last night?

"You know . . . ," Sierra began slowly, talking to all three of us but looking right at me. "It sounds crazy. But Ryun was able to make last night the best Christmas Eve I think I've ever had. This accident is bringing us closer together than ever."

"That is so beautiful!" gushed Carin. "So? Tell all! What did Ryun give you?"

Sierra seemed to think about this. "Okay," she finally said. "One gift, I *can* show you. But one I can't."

"I *love* this!" Carin exclaimed.

I just stood there, staring without speaking. I felt Holly glancing at me, as if she suspected all was not well. Still, I tried to maintain a poker face, although I'd never been good at poker and was sure I was losing now.

Sierra pulled out the mystery novel and said, "Isn't Ryun thoughtful? He knows I love mysteries. Plus, the card was so sweet."

Ryun didn't mention a card. But then why would he?

"And the *other* present?" Carin was using her best coaxing voice. "You *have* to tell. Right, girls?"

"That's up to Sierra." Holly looked like she was getting bored with this game.

I could feel Sierra looking at me, but I just pretended to be interested in a giant pink poinsettia that was next to her bed.

"Okay. I'll hint," continued Sierra in a mysterious voice. "Let's just say it's red. And I've got it on right now."

I turned in time to see her pulling her robe around her modestly.

"Victoria's Secret!" Carin squealed.

Then, to my relief, Holly cut in. "I have to get home. My mom's freaking that I cut out of Christmas so fast. Great seeing you, Sierra."

Carin went on for a while about how cool it must've been to have amnesia, and I felt like telling her I'd be happy to knock her in the head and let her give it a go. But I controlled myself and waited a couple of minutes before I said, "We gotta go." I waved to Sierra and headed for the door.

"Yeah. Merry Christmas, Sierra," Holly called out as she joined me by the door.

"Thanks for coming," Sierra called in a happy voice, but her eyes narrowed. "And for the shirt."

And then Holly and I just split.

"Let Carin ride the bus home," said Holly as we headed for the elevator.

But we were barely to the lobby when Carin

came running up from behind us. "What's the big hurry, you guys?" she demanded.

"It's Christmas, Carin," said Holly. "I promised my family I'd stick around."

"Yeah, me too," I echoed. And suddenly the thought of hanging with my dumpy and frumpy and less-than-fashionable family sounded like a real holiday to me.

21

I tried to act as if nothing was wrong when Ryun showed up on my doorstep later that same day. And although we'd previously planned to get together on Christmas to exchange our gifts, I hadn't completely expected him to come.

I was silent as I got into his Explorer. And seething. The more I thought about the "red Victoria's Secret" item, the angrier I got. I knew then that I'd been playing the fool and it was about time I put an end to it.

"How was your visit with Sierra?" he asked innocently.

"How do you think it was?" I tossed back.

"What do you mean?"

"What do you think I mean?"

We were sitting in the Explorer at the park now,

just a neighborhood park, but quiet and private with lots of trees around.

"You're acting kind of crazy, Kenzie," said Ryun softly. "Everything okay?"

"No, everything is *not* okay."

He held up his hands now. "Just tell me what's going on, please. I'm not into playing games today."

"Why don't you tell me what's going on, Ryun?" I demanded. "You didn't!"

"I didn't what?" He looked totally confused now.

This guy is good. He can put on quite the show, I thought. "Your present to Sierra!"

"You mean the book?" he said. "P. D. James was your idea. Why are you getting so bent . . ."

I got out of his SUV and slammed the door loudly for emphasis. If I was going to get mad, I might as well make a good scene. Just the same, I was relieved that the park was deserted. I wasn't looking for spectators.

Ryun got out of the Explorer too. He didn't look happy.

"*Not* P. D. James!" I yelled. "The *other* present, the one Sierra wouldn't show us when we went by to see her."

"What other present?" He acted totally baffled now. Almost convincing. Almost. "I only gave her the P. D. James novel, like you and I had talked about."

I stared at him, trying to figure out whether he was an extremely good liar or I was going totally nuts. "So you didn't give her something *red from Victoria's Secret?*" I said, seething.

And then he had the audacity to laugh at me. *"Victoria's Secret?* Are you crazy?"

Now *I* was totally confused, like I was the brunt of a bad joke, the loser in a game where the rules were always changing. What was going on? "But Sierra said you'd gotten her something red, underneath her hospital clothes. . . ."

"Did she show it to you?"

I considered this. "Well, no, she didn't actually show it to us. Carin and Holly were there too. But she was about to."

"But she *didn't* show it to you?"

"No, I guess not."

Ryun seemed to relax now. "Okay, then I'm telling you. I *didn't* give her something from Victoria's Secret or anything else. It was just P. D. James. Nothing else."

I still wasn't totally sure. Nothing seemed to make much sense right now. "But why would Sierra tell us she'd gotten something like that from you when she didn't?"

Ryun just shrugged. "Who knows? Maybe she was mad she was stuck in the hospital on Christmas Eve. And because I gave her some book. I'm sure she would have liked something a little nicer." Then he got this sneaky look in his eyes as he reached into the inside pocket of his coat. "Speaking of something nicer . . ."

My anger began to melt as I waited for him to hand me a small blue velvet box, not the square kind that a ring might come in, but a flat rectangular one. Even so I was excited. "What is it?" I asked eagerly.

"Open it and see."

So I opened the box to discover an exquisite pearl hanging on a delicate gold chain. "It's beautiful!" I gasped.

"And it's for you." Then he helped me put on the necklace and stepped back to look at it. He took me into his arms and gave me a hug.

Everything is going to be okay after all, I thought.

"I have something for you too," I told him. But now my gift didn't feel very special, at least not compared to his. Just the same I dug down in my coat pocket for the small wrapped package. I waited for him to tear off the handmade paper, an art project at Little Lambs last week.

He held up the brass soccer ball key chain and grinned. "Cool."

"It's not much," I apologized.

"I love it," he assured me. "And it will go with me everywhere I go."

We started to walk around the park.

"I'm sorry," I said, feeling like the world's worst heel. How could I ever have doubted him?

"So you trust me?"

"Yes, I trust you," I told him, still feeling slightly confused about all that had happened.

■   ■   ■

I wasn't sure why Sierra pulled that little stunt on Christmas, but I decided I couldn't trust her anymore. Maybe the blow to her head changed her personality. I'd heard that can happen. People who were uptight and mean suddenly turn sweet and kind. And people who were happy and easygoing turn into real grumps. I wondered if that was what happened to Sierra. Or did she know? Did she remember something?

Whatever it was, I avoided her the next week. I didn't stop by the hospital once. I told Ryun to explain that I was working extra hours at Little Lambs, which was true. But I knew I could make time to see her if I wanted to. I just didn't want to. Then Ryun called and said she was really sick.

"She's running a high fever," he told me, sounding concerned. "They were going to release her, but now they've got to keep her longer."

"That's too bad."

"Yeah, maybe you should stop in or something."

Why should I have to go visit her? I thought, but I kept that to myself. The less Ryun and I discussed Sierra, the happier we were. Just the same, I decided to give her a call.

"How are you doing?" I asked.

"A little better."

"That's good." I strained my brain to come up with something to say. "I've been working extra hours at Little Lambs. We try to keep the doors open during the holidays since some of our families can get pretty stressed during this time. Otherwise I would've come to visit you more." I knew it sounded lame, but it was the best I could do.

"That's okay, Kenzie. I understand. Did I tell you about the gorgeous bouquet Ryun got for me?" She laughed. "It must've cost a fortune."

"That's nice," I said quickly and probably too sharply.

"Yeah, it is nice."

I made an excuse to get off the phone and resisted the urge to throw something after I hung up. Why was she doing this to me? Or could it be true? I told myself it was another lie and decided not to even mention it to Ryun. Especially since he'd planned a special date for New Year's Eve. And after the way I acted on Christmas, I knew I needed to trust him more.

"Where are we going?" I asked as he drove away from my house.

"It's a surprise."

"Cool." It was beginning to snow now and everything was looking like a fairyland, all coated in white frosting that glimmered in the streetlights.

"Did you hear that Sierra went home today?"

"Seriously?"

"Yeah, I guess her temperature finally went down."

"Well, that's good."

We finally ended up at a little Chinese restaurant called Chan's at the edge of town. I'd seen it before, but it always looked a little seedy and no one in my family really liked Chinese food anyway.

"Don't be fooled," Ryun whispered as we went inside. "This might be a *Chinese* restaurant, but my aunt's the one who runs it, and she's really Korean." He laughed. "Just don't tell anyone."

"Why doesn't she run a Korean restaurant?" I asked as a young man who obviously recognized Ryun seated us at a cozy corner table in the back.

I noticed that our table seemed to be fixed up extra nice, with some New Year's decorations and several candles.

"Because no one likes Korean food," said Ryun as he winked at the waiter.

"What about Koreans?" I asked.

He laughed. "Well, some of them might like it, but my aunt learned that you can make more money with a Chinese restaurant."

"But how does she know how to make Chinese food if she's Korean?"

"She doesn't. She just hires Chinese cooks."

I nodded. "I see." Then I picked up a party popper. "Looks like someone's having a party."

He smiled and took my hand. "I told my aunt I was bringing someone special."

We had a fantastic time and were treated like royalty. By the end of the night I realized I actually liked Chinese food. Most of the other diners, not that there were many to start with, were long gone by midnight, so several of Ryun's relatives joined us for a little impromptu New Year's celebration. It was like a private party. I couldn't remember when I'd had as much fun.

22

I was shocked but pleased to see Sierra back at school on the first day after winter break. She hobbled toward us on her crutch, a cluster of friends hovering around her as if she were a celebrity. I guess in a way she was.

I tried not to act as if I'd been caught in the act. After all, Ryun and I were only standing by the lockers just innocently talking. No crime in that. But judging by the look in Sierra's eye, I wasn't so sure. But then I forced a smile to my face, greeted her, and even carried her books. Her idea, not mine. Not that I didn't want to help her, I did. But I felt awkward being with both Sierra and Ryun at the same time, like I was the intruder, the fifth wheel. I tried to ignore those feelings as we walked to class together. I kept telling myself it wouldn't be like this forever.

Besides, I still felt sorry for Sierra. She looked
a lot better than she did right after the wreck, but
in some ways she seemed like just a shadow of the
old Sierra. And I really missed the old Sierra. We
used to have a good time together. I wished I could
have her back.

In the meantime I followed her around whenever
I could, helping her with her books and her crutch
and whatever. I was her personal slave, and it seemed
like she was enjoying it a little too much. Sometimes
I even got the impression she'd like me to bow down
and pay her homage, but then I may be exaggerat-
ing. Still I began to think of her as Queen Sierra. I
would never say as much, of course, but I thought
I was her lackey.

■   ■   ■

By midweek, I was getting a little sick of the game.
But I told myself, although it wasn't easy, I *could*
do this. I *would* do this. I was determined to play
the faithful friend to Sierra—at least for a while.
And I'd be happy to be a genuine friend to her if
it was possible to erase all that had gone on between
us this year. I guess I'd hoped her amnesia had provided the perfect eraser. That we could return to
what used to be. But now I wasn't so sure. Something felt different. Maybe it was just me, acting
all hypersensitive and paranoid, but it seemed like
she couldn't talk about her relationship with Ryun
enough to me. Every time I turned around she was
going on and on about how wonderful Ryun was

and how he was so totally devoted to her. By the end of the week I was seriously bummed.

"It's so amazing," she gushed as we waited for Ryun to join us between classes on Friday. "Ever since the accident, it's as if we just keep getting closer and closer. He calls me all the time and even my mom talks to him." She smiled and waved as he approached, then threw her arms around him and kissed him.

I turned away and literally bit my tongue.

Somehow I made it through the rest of that day and the ongoing assault of Sierra's very public demonstrations of affection toward Ryun without hurling. But it was an act of supreme self-control and something I knew I couldn't carry off forever.

Finally, when I thought I could make a gracious exit, I excused myself and headed for the nearest exit.

Ryun was waiting for me at the bike rack.

"How did you get here so fast?" I demanded as I bent down to undo my lock.

"Took a shortcut while you went to your locker." He rubbed his knee now.

"Did you hurt yourself?" I asked, standing up to look at his face.

"Probably went a little faster than I should've." He smiled at me now. "But I just wanted to see you before you left. I wanted to say you're really being brave about all this."

I just shrugged and slipped the straps of my backpack over my shoulders. "Aren't you worried someone might see us out here? Get the wrong idea again?"

"We can't keep this up forever."

"But we have to keep it up for a while." I surprised myself. *Now I'm the one who wants to continue the charade?*

"It's going to unravel eventually."

"But it's too soon," I told him. "Everyone still feels sorry for Sierra. If you break up with her now, it'll look bad. Like you don't want to be with her because she looks different or something."

He shook his head. "I don't know . . ."

"Well, I do," I said with fresh resolve. "We've got to keep this up for at least another week."

He groaned.

"Come on, Ryun," I urged him. "You know we have to."

He nodded. "You're right. But all I want to do is be with you, babe."

Relief washed over me. "Yeah, me too. But let's just make sure we do this thing right this time."

I felt like singing as I pedaled off to work. I was sure that, in spite of all Sierra's claims of Ryun's undying devotion, he really loved me. And suddenly I thought, *I can keep this secret for a while longer now.*

Even with everything I'd gone through this winter, I had always tried to act positive and cheerful at work—for the sake of the kids. But today it felt like the real thing. And the kids seemed to know it as we sang songs like "If You're Happy and You Know It" during our music session. By the time my shift was done, I felt like maybe my life had finally taken a turn. Maybe I would make it through this thing—and safely to the other side.

I put on an upbeat CD as I puttered around in my room, laying out a cool outfit to wear to the game that night. Never mind that I had to go solo. I told myself that I was a big girl and I could go to the game alone. I could meet my friends once I was there and still have a good time. I imagined myself joking and laughing with Holly and Carin and the others, carefully keeping my eyes away from Ryun and Sierra. Of course, I'd hang with the "happy couple" too, but I would keep my distance. I'd put on a good show to convince everyone that Ryun and I were nothing more than just friends.

Then the phone rang. Since it didn't sound like Lark was picking it up, I ran to get it. It was Ryun. I was surprised when he asked me to go to the game with him.

"What?" I demanded. "But how can we–?"

"It's okay," he assured me. "Sierra has begged out."

"You're kidding?"

"No, she said she's not feeling too great. She just wants to stay home and take it easy."

"But maybe you should go and be with her."

He laughed. "Wow, Kenzie, you are really something. Actually encouraging me to go be with Sierra instead of you."

"Well, that's not what I meant . . . exactly." I considered the situation. "It's just that I don't want to stir things up, you know."

"It's okay. We'll just be going as friends."

"But what will everybody say?"

"Why should they say anything?"

"Because that's how it works."

"Look, we'll just act like we're both missing Sierra and keeping each other company. No biggie."

Finally I agreed, but I wasn't sure it was such a smart move. But I did look forward to being at the game with Ryun—without Sierra sitting between us. I was just worried we were moving too fast.

Even so, I made sure to put together the best-looking outfit. I wished I could get Sierra's input, since her taste was absolutely impeccable. But I could just hear myself calling her and asking, "Hey, Sierra, what do you think would look really hot on me tonight, since I'm going to the basketball game with your boyfriend?" Yeah, you bet!

Finally I decided on a red sweater that I got at the Gap last fall. Sierra had said it really showed off my curves. I paired this with my best flare jeans and my Steve Madden boots and thought, *I actually do look pretty hot.* I was glad I'd taken the time to get my hair touched up last week.

"Got a date?" asked Lark as I skipped downstairs.

"No," I told her. "Just going to the game with a friend."

She frowned. "I don't know why you keep acting like you and Ryun are *just* friends. It's pretty ridiculous."

"Huh?" I'd never told Lark anything about Ryun and me.

"Everyone knows, Kenzie."

"Really?"

"Well, everyone in this family. It's not like we're blind. Oh, maybe Aaron and Josh don't suspect anything. But I'm sure Mom and Dad are onto you."

"We're just friends, Lark."

"Yeah, and I'm going out with Brad Pitt."

I was frustrated. I'd just been caught by my kid sister. "Look, Lark, Ryun and Sierra are still an item, if you know what I mean."

"Ya think." She rolled her eyes. "Of course he has to stick it out with her for a while, just to make it look good. I'm not stupid, you know."

"Right."

"So who are you going to the game with tonight?"

"Actually, Ryun is giving me a ride, but—"

Lark threw back her head and laughed. "See, Kenzie, I was right."

I frowned at her, then went into the kitchen, where Mom was heating up an enormous pan of lasagna. "Smells good," I told her.

"You going out?" She eyed my outfit.

"To the game."

"With Ryun?"

"What is it with you people?" I demanded.

Mom laughed. "Maybe it's the look on your face. But tell me, honey, did Ryun and Sierra break up?"

"No, they didn't break up. Sierra just happened to beg out of the game tonight since she's not feeling well. And Ryun is giving me a ride. That's all," I said firmly.

Mom nodded but looked unconvinced. "Well, be careful, Kenzie."

"Careful?"

"Well, it could look wrong for you and Ryun to be together at the game when Sierra isn't with you."

I sighed. "We're just friends, Mom."

degrees of betrayal

23

It was incredibly fun being at the game with Ryun. I even thought of it as a real date, although I did a pretty good job of watching my step and acting as if we were *just friends* and nothing more. I'd already told Carin and Holly that I had planned to come with Sierra and Ryun tonight but that Sierra wasn't feeling well . . . and Ryun gave me a ride since I didn't have anyone else to call. I think they believed me, although you could never tell with Holly. But then she'd been pretty loyal to me throughout this whole mess.

Then I must have temporarily forgotten where I was because before I realized what was happening I was leaning into Ryun and we were holding hands—just as if we were all alone at the park with no one around. The problem was *everyone* was around. We were sitting in a jam-packed gym with a couple thousand sets of eyes all around us.

And at least one camera. Of course, it didn't look like a camera, since it was carefully disguised as a cell phone. Ryun was the one who noticed this clever trick. And when he did, he ripped his hand away from me so fast that I felt like I was poison. Then he nodded to where Carin was standing down below and aiming her new Christmas present straight at us.

"What?" I asked nervously. *"What* is she doing?"

Ryun leaned over to whisper in my ear. "Carin saw us holding hands."

I peered back down to Carin. She was with Greg and he was intently watching the game. But she was intently looking at her cell phone now, like she was still doing something with it. I was afraid that Ryun was right.

"Do you think she'll tell Sierra?" I asked, knowing full well that Carin was loyal to Sierra.

"I think she took a picture of us," he said.

And, of course, he was right. It was only a matter of time before everyone had seen the picture of Ryun and me, holding hands at the basketball game. Smile—you're on candid camera.

By the time I got home, the e-mail was already flying back and forth across the Highview cyberspace. Thankfully, my parents had gone to bed and Lark was actually spending the night at Lacy's—after a full week of begging my mom.

So I had the family room and the computer all to myself. Naturally Holly forwarded me the "revealing" photo. It wasn't too bad. I actually printed it out. It was cool to see what we looked like together.

Of course, the problem was, we'd been "caught in the act," even though it seemed innocent to me. We were only holding hands. Maybe I could make everybody believe that Ryun was consoling me about something. I decided to try. I sent out several e-mails carefully explaining this, making up a lie about how I got into a big fight with my parents over college. I ended it by saying that Ryun and I were "just friends." I did everything I could to reassure Sierra that it wasn't what it appeared to be, and even to convince her we'd be totally stupid to show up like that in public if we *were* really seriously involved. Of course, I was thinking, *We really* are *stupid,* even as I hit the send button.

But Sierra didn't respond to any of my e-mails.

■ ■ ■

I went to church with my family on Sunday again. I guess I was hoping that God might have mercy on me and help me through my most recent crisis. Then, of all things, Pastor Ken talked about Adam and Eve. How Sunday school was that? Man, I'd been subjected to that story since I was in diapers. Eve blew it by eating the banned apple, and then, not wanting to suffer alone, she offered it to Adam. God got mad and banished them from Eden. Yada-yada, blah, blah, blah.

But today Pastor Ken was taking a different approach. I tried to distract myself by doodling on

---

the blank spaces in the bulletin, but I couldn't help but listen. Pastor Ken was saying that the problem in Paradise was that Adam and Eve lied to God.

"You see, God must've known they were going to blow it," he said. "After all, he *is* God. He *knows* everything. But Scripture says that God created man to have a *relationship* with him. He wanted to be *friends* with Adam and Eve. To walk through the garden and enjoy their company, to talk with them and discuss the events of the day. Like what did you name that funny long-necked and spotted animal?"

The congregation chuckled, and I leaned forward to listen more closely.

"But we all know that a relationship deteriorates when one party is dishonest. Lies separate us from each other. They separate us from God."

I leaned back in the pew. It felt like he was talking directly to me, and it made me nervous. Still, I'd gotten better and better at playing it cool, and I tried to play it cool again. Just the same, I wondered if someone had tipped Pastor Ken off about my web of lies. But he acted oblivious to me as he continued talking about how God knows our hearts and above all wants honesty from us.

"Our dishonesty is what drives us away from God," he said. "Remember how Adam and Eve hid from God, even before they knew how he was going to react? It was because they were ashamed about what they'd done. Our lies make us ashamed to come to God. They can destroy our friendship with him."

And in that moment I knew—with the same kind of clarity that I knew my own name—that I had done exactly that. I had allowed my lies to destroy my relationship with God. I knew that he knew I was a big fat liar. Finally, Pastor Ken led us in a prayer of confession, encouraging us to admit that we all have some form of dishonesty in our lives and inviting God to examine our hearts and cleanse us. But even though I longed to make things right, I couldn't say this prayer with the rest of the congregation. As crazy as it seemed, I refused to be a hypocrite again. Because I knew it was a promise I couldn't keep. I knew I wouldn't be able to show up at school tomorrow and come clean. And I didn't want to lie to God again and tell him I would. So instead I asked God to help me find my way out of this mess. Okay, it wasn't much. But this time I really meant it.

24

As I walked into school on Monday, I felt as if I were going to my own execution. I wondered if my friends, rather ex-friends, might be so kind as to give me a blindfold. Or a cigarette, but I don't smoke. I felt the stares, heard the whispers, as I made my way to my locker. But I stared straight ahead and held my head high. The only one who would talk to me was Holly and even she seemed a little irked.

"It was a stupid move," she told me for like the hundredth time.

"I know," I said. "But it wasn't like it seemed."

"Yeah, sure." She rolled her eyes at me. "Try convincing Carin."

Carin spent the whole day ingratiating herself to Sierra by denouncing me to everyone who would listen. No big surprises there, especially since she and Sierra had been friends since grade school. But even more than that, Carin *loved* being the center of attention, which happened to be right by Sierra's side at the moment.

By afternoon, I was telling myself that maybe it was all for the best. Maybe Ryun and I could just come out of the closet, so to speak, and admit that we did like each other. As in, *get over it*, everyone. And I knew they would. In time. Of course, it might be a very long time. But even so, I was ready to end this game. I looked forward to walking with Ryun down the hall, holding hands, and laughing. Going to games and dances and parties together. Maybe all this grief would be worth it.

But by the end of the day, the tables had turned again and I wondered, *Just who is running this game, anyway? Is it you, God?* I learned by way of Holly, who heard it from Carin, that Ryun and Sierra had patched things up!

How? I wondered. How on earth did they patch things up? And why now? Just when I thought we might be able to end this thing once and for all. Oh, man, I was so sick and tired of being jerked around.

Then to make matters worse, Sierra called that night. "I just wanted to let you know that everything's okay," she said smoothly.

"What does that mean, exactly?" I asked.

"It means that Ryun explained everything to me." She laughed lightly. "And it's obvious that he feels nothing for you."

"Nothing?" I hated the mousy sound of my voice.

"Of course, he thinks of you as a friend," she continued. "Especially since you're such a good friend to me, Kenzie. I mean, you were one of the few people who came to see me in the hospital. You've been so loyal to me. And it only seems fair that my boyfriend should be able to get along with my *best* friend, don't you think?"

I didn't say anything. I was too stunned to speak. Was she serious about the best friend part? Even with all that had gone on, I still wished that was true.

"So, really, Kenzie, don't worry about a thing. Ryun and I are just fine. Perfectly fine. And he has totally assured me that his love for me is real and that he'd never do anything to hurt me." She laughed again. "We had a really good time kissing and making up. I guess that makes a little spat like this all the more worthwhile."

"Right." My voice was flat now.

"So, no hard feelings, really."

"Right."

"See ya tomorrow." And then she hung up.

Just quit, I told myself as I returned the phone to the kitchen. I smacked my fist on the counter, then glanced around to see if anyone was around to see me. Fortunately they were all in the family room. But I was so angry that I wasn't sure I could keep myself under control.

Just give up! I told myself as I headed for the door. *It's not worth it. Ryun isn't worth it. Sierra isn't worth it.* Even though it was dark and cold, I stormed out of the house, furious at what was happening to me. It was like everything was totally out of control. My whole life.

I felt like a helpless marionette where someone else got to pull all the strings. Someone would pull a string, and *boom,* I would punch myself in the nose. Then another string, and *bam,* I would whack myself on the head. It was ridiculous, really, but it was how I felt.

Before I knew it, I was walking in the deserted park, stomping around like a crazy girl. I fumed and vented, desperately wishing that—*presto-chango!*—I could just turn into someone else. I remembered how, with Holly's help, I had rein-vented myself last summer. I wondered if it was possible to do it again.

And then I heard him calling my name. "Kenzie?"

I turned to see Ryun coming toward me. I felt torn. Part of me wanted to run to him, to fall in his arms and sob. Part of me wanted to turn and run the other way. And another part of me wanted to lash into him.

"Are you okay?"

I just stood and stared at him, not sure of what the correct answer might be tonight. And if I got it right, would I win the prize, or would someone smack me down again? "I don't know," I finally said, which at least was true.

"I called your house and Lark told me that you were upset."

"Lark?" Had my little sister been spying on me?

"She said you'd just taken off on foot and that you looked really mad."

"She did?" Maybe Lark was more perceptive than I thought.

Then he told me that everything he said to Sierra this afternoon was just to "smooth things over."

"That's not what it sounded like to me," I fired back.

"It's true," he said. "I was only trying to buy us some time."

"Buy us some time by declaring your undying affection to Sierra?"

"That's not how it—"

"How could you?" I folded my arms across my chest and shivered. I was so mad I'd forgotten my coat.

"But I didn't."

"Sierra said it, for a fact," I told him hotly. "You *told* her you love her. Not only that, but even before that she's been telling me how you guys have been talking a lot since the accident. And that since she got back from the hospital, you are getting closer and closer."

"Kenzie, you know it isn't true . . ."

"I don't know anything anymore," I sobbed, holding my clenched fists in the air as if I'd like to hit him.

"You're cold," he said gently. Then he removed his jacket and slipped it over my shoulders. "And you're upset." He put his arms around me and pulled me toward him. I felt myself melting, giving in, letting someone else pull the strings again.

"But Sierra said—"

202

"Sierra said—Sierra said," he repeated. "Can't we just forget what Sierra said?"

"But she really believes you love her, Ryun."
I continued to hold my still-clenched fists between us, almost as if I were protecting myself.

"That doesn't make it true," he told me, pulling me even closer.

Doesn't make it true? I thought. *But what is true? It's almost as if I can't tell the difference between the truth and the lies anymore. Everything feels murky and gray.*

degrees of betrayal

"We need to talk," Mom told me after church, the Sunday before Valentine's Day. She had just gotten home from a meeting with the Little Lambs board, and she sounded serious.

"Sure," I said. "What about?"

"Come into the family room," she said. When Lark got up to follow, she waved my sister back.

"What?" I demanded. "What is it?"

"There's been a complaint."

"A complaint?" I sat down in a chair. "About what?"

"About you."

"About me?"

Mom nodded.

"What do you mean? What kind of complaint?"

"The board has decided to do an investigation," she said.

"About what? What on earth are you talking about, Mom?" I was back on my feet now. "What's going on?"

"You tell me, honey." She eyed me.

"Tell you what?" Suddenly it hit me. Mom knew about the wreck, that Ryun was the driver that night, that I hadn't told the police the whole truth . . . "What do you mean?" I asked weakly.

"Is it true," she began, "that you have been doing drugs?"

"Drugs?" I repeated, not sure I'd heard her right.

"Yes. Drugs." Her eyes probed me now, as if she could figure out the truth just by looking.

"Mom," I began in my most serious voice, "of course not. You know I don't do drugs. That would be so incredibly stupid."

She seemed a little relieved but not completely convinced. "But you've changed a lot this year, McKenzie. You've made different friends, you don't go to youth group anymore, and you've been, well, moody."

Who wouldn't be moody if they had to live my life? I thought.

"And someone informed a member of the board that you're involved in drugs and drinking and—" She held up her hands. "Who knows what else?"

I could see she was close to tears. "But it's not true, Mom," I told her. "I have never done drugs."

"Never?"

"Never, I swear to you. I have never done drugs."

"Are you willing to take a drug test?"

"Of course."

She nodded. "But what about the drinking?"

I paused. I'd had an occasional beer at a party, but what kid hasn't? I tried to decide which route to take, then chose to be honest. "I don't really drink, as a rule," I told her. "But sometimes I'll have a beer, just to fit in, Mom. Just because my friends are all drinking."

She looked seriously disappointed.

"It's not that big of a deal," I tried to assure her. "I don't even like it. And if it makes you feel any better, I won't do it again."

"Oh, McKenzie."

"I'm sorry, Mom."

"It's just that I run Little Lambs, honey. And you are my daughter and the board trusted you with your new role here at Little Lambs . . . and now this."

"I'm really sorry," I said again. "But what can I do?"

She shook her head. "I don't know. It's just that this, well, this scandal puts everything at risk here."

"What do you mean?"

"Well, now the board wants to investigate everything."

"What do you mean by everything?"

"Oh, they just got going about how dangerous it is to have someone in charge who hires her own children as employees—"

"You mean they're accusing you of—"

"Not accusing exactly. But they used words like *nepotism*—"

206

"Like they think our family is going to take over Little Lambs?" I had to laugh.

"It's not funny, McKenzie."

"It's ridiculous, Mom. Here you are, giving your heart and soul to this place, just so you can help some of the disadvantaged kids in the neighborhood, and they're accusing you of nepotism?"

"Well, it wasn't quite that bad. They just want to go over everything very carefully—the books and the budget and . . ." She sighed. "Everything."

"I'm really sorry."

"It's not that I'm worried, honey. I haven't done anything wrong. I have nothing to hide. It's just that it makes for a lot of extra work."

"And embarrassment," I added.

She didn't say anything, but I noticed a couple of tears slipping down her cheeks. I felt horrible, like this was totally my fault. As I put my hand on her shoulder and made a feeble attempt to comfort her, I wondered why this was happening to us. Who would go to the board with this kind of accusation about me?

"Mom? Who told the board that I was doing drugs?"

She shrugged. "I don't know. I'm sure it was an anonymous complaint."

"But how can someone just say something like that—something that's a total lie—anonymously?"

"I don't know, honey." She pushed some newspapers aside. "It's just the way the board works, I guess."

"But it's not fair."

degrees of betrayal

"Life's not fair," she said in a tired voice.

"So I have to prove to them I'm innocent?"

"Yes."

"Guilty until proven innocent."

"Apparently." She sighed.

"Well, that'll be easy," I told her. "I'll just do the drug test and that will be the end of it. Right?"

"Not necessarily," she said. "Yes, you'll do the drug test. But the board will have to see the results and then they'll schedule a meeting to question you . . ."

"And everything will be fine," I finished for her.

"Hopefully."

"Where do I get a drug test?" I asked.

"We'll call the doctor."

I nodded. "Okay."

But she still looked crushed.

"I still go to work after school tomorrow, though, right?"

She shook her head. "The board has requested that you step aside, McKenzie."

"What?"

"Just until the investigation is complete and until they make their decision."

"But that's not fair."

She gave me the look—the one I knew meant *life's not fair*.

"So I'm fired?" I said. "Just like that?"

"Not fired, honey, just—"

"This is wrong, Mom," I told her. "I know it's not your fault, but it stinks. And it's totally wrong. Those kids in there love me, and they're going to miss me, and—" My eyes filled with tears. "And I'm going to miss them."

"I'm sorry, honey."

"Does this mean I'll miss the Valentine's Day trip?" I asked. Every year we took the kids up to stay at a lodge and play in the snow for either the weekend before or after Valentine's Day. It was coming up soon—in fact, the very next weekend. It was one of the highlights of the year.

"Unless the investigation is finished by then," my mom said wearily. "And only if you're cleared."

"Cleared?" I exploded. "It's all just a stupid lie!"

Then I stormed out of the family room and out of the house, with tears practically blinding me.

Eventually I ended up at the park and just walked. I walked and walked and walked, going around and around on the trail that only went in a circle. I felt like a dog chasing his tail as I tried to make sense of this whole mess.

Finally, I stopped at a park bench and sat down. Putting my head in my hands, I began to sob. And I sobbed and sobbed and sobbed. And the more I sobbed, the more I thought I'd never be able to stop.

But finally I did. I wiped my face on the sleeve of my jacket and took in a raggedy breath. And then I looked up at the somber gray sky and I said, "God, I'm sorry. I'm sorry about everything. I want to make things right. I just don't know how."

I sat and waited, hoping that God would answer me. Maybe he'd even write something profound across the sky. But he didn't.

kenzie's story

Feeling totally betrayed by the false accusations that had been made to the board, I knew I could no longer trust *anyone* at school. So I kept to myself on the following Monday.

I was at my locker when Ryun called, "Kenzie?"

I took a book out of my locker, then closed it. I glanced up at him only for a second because my eyes were red from crying. I just didn't want to talk, so I hurried down the hall toward lit class and sat in the back, with my head in a book. As soon as the bell rang, I was out of there.

But Ryun caught up with me before I got to my next class. "What is it?" he asked. "Are you okay?"

"What do you care?" I tossed back.

Now he looked really hurt and I felt guilty. "I care about *you*," he told me. "What's going on with you, Kenzie?"

"I'll tell you what's been going on." My voice was low, and I could hear the anger in it. *"Somebody* told the Little Lambs board that I was drinking and taking drugs. I may have lost my job."

I couldn't help myself. I started to cry.

"But you don't do any of that stuff," Ryun said, looking puzzled.

"It doesn't matter. They're investigating me, and I might never be able to go back. I can't even help with the Valentine's trip this weekend."

"I'm sorry, Kenzie." He reached for my hand. "I didn't know."

"No, I didn't think so. Maybe it's because you've been so involved in Sierra's perfect little life. How can you have time to know what's going on in mine? Well, let me tell you, Ryun, it's messed up. Totally messed up."

I started crying again, only harder this time. Ryun tried to put his arm around me, but I shrugged it off and took off toward the john.

The rest of the day I avoided all of my so-called friends, escaped all conversations including "hi" or "hey." I didn't go to the cafeteria for lunch after fourth period, and even though I had no job to go to, I cut out of there right after my last class and headed straight home.

I felt totally rotten. I couldn't help but think, *Who am I anymore? Or who am I becoming?* It was scary. Like I was on this track, going 100 miles an hour, and there was no way to get off. Would I just have to crash and burn?

Once I got home, I saw a note on the counter.

Mom had scheduled a drug test for me at the hospital that afternoon at 2:00. I had an hour before I had to leave.

I went straight to my room and got into bed.

"Why are you doing this to me?" I asked God out loud, as if he were personally to blame. I knew he wasn't. I knew it was all my fault, that I was just reaping all the crud and lies and stupidity that I'd sowed since the summer before my senior year.

"Are you *ever* going to help me, God?" I pleaded. "I told you I was sorry," I reminded him. "I told you I'd try to fix everything . . . if I only knew how. I just don't know how . . . or what to do. I feel like I'm in prison, and I don't know how to get out. Please help me."

But God didn't say anything, and I still had to go to the hospital.

So an hour later I was sitting in the waiting area, next to a woman and her little boy who was acting kind of cranky. I felt sorry for the young mom, who didn't seem much older than me. And since I'd had some experience around kids, I offered to read him a story from the pile of tattered picture books on the table. When it was her turn to go in for her lab test, she asked if I'd mind keeping an eye on him. Surprised she would trust a perfect stranger, I agreed and managed to keep him occupied for the next 10 minutes.

The mother returned and took her little boy just before a stocky nurse, who looked like she could be in the military, informed me that it was my turn. She told me to come around the side of the desk

and then insisted I remove my coat, hooded sweat-shirt, and backpack. I felt like I was being frisked as she eyeballed me and even told me to take off my boots. Finally satisfied that I was carrying no contraband—what else could it be?—she handed me a cup and pointed me toward the bathroom. I almost expected her to say, "March! Left, right—left, right—left!"

Feeling like a junkie who's gotten caught, I went inside the bathroom, locked the door, then searched around the brightly lit room for a secret camera. It had to be somewhere. Maybe it was tucked into the fan or the lights or behind the one-way glass mirror? I stood there for several minutes, just looking around like I really was guilty of something.

Finally, I told myself to stop being ridiculous, and I relaxed enough to actually "deposit my sample" in their stupid plastic cup. I secured the lid of the cup, flushed the toilet, washed my hands, and then walked out of the bathroom feeling totally degraded. I knew that everyone in the waiting room was staring at me, knowing I was being tested for drugs, as I handed Nurse Sourpuss my little white cup.

Then I scrambled to redress myself, actually getting my arm stuck in the twisted sleeve of my coat, before I rushed out of that place in complete embarrassment. I was so angry when I left that if I'd known who was responsible, who had lied to the board, I would have hunted that person down and caused some serious damage!

The next day, Tuesday, it didn't help that it was Valentine's Day. Everyone seemed to have romance on the brain. It was like a disease. Most of my so-called friends were going as couples, of course, to The Lantern that night. Naturally, they would only go to Highview's most premiere and expensive restaurant. What else would do to *celebrate their love?* Gag me!

And Ryun and Sierra were one of those couples. I tried not to let it bug me, but it did.

But, true to form, Ryun came through again. He managed to slip a couple of sweet notes into my locker. One even had a poem.

"I'm really, really sorry, Kenzie," he told me today. "I had no idea things were so bad for you."

"Yeah . . ." I felt myself softening toward him again. It was like I couldn't resist this guy—*Ryun, the guy I love.*

"I brought you something." He reached into his backpack to pull out what looked like a slightly crumpled box of chocolates and a card. "This is for you."

"Thanks." I hurried to hide the items in my backpack, worried that someone might see this little transaction and get suspicious.

"You're the one I want to be with, Kenzie," he told me. "If I could have it my way, you'd be the one having dinner with me at The Lantern tonight."

I really didn't want to start crying. Not here at school. Not in front of him. But I was really close. "It's just so hard," I finally managed to say.

"I know."

When he took my hand and gazed into my eyes, I believed him. "Oh, Ryun," I said. "I'm so sick and tired of this game."

He touched my cheek. "So am I," he said quietly. "But, really, Kenzie, it's almost over. I just didn't think it'd look good to break up with Sierra right before Valentine's Day, you know."

I nodded. "I know you're right. It's just been really hard lately."

"I want to be with you, Kenzie." He leaned forward and his lips brushed my cheek.

"And I want to be with you," I admitted.

"It won't be long . . . I promise."

Part of me believed him. But another part of me still wondered if Ryun might really love Sierra more than me. But every single time I was finally ready to spill the beans—to come clean—I remembered something. I could get into big trouble with the police for not telling the whole truth, but Ryun would take even more heat. The consequences could be really serious for him.

And then my heart would begin to take over again. Then I'd tell myself that this was about *Ryun and me* and about preserving what we had so we could finally be together. Maybe forever.

And then there was the whole God thing. I kept remembering those things I'd heard in church my whole life—like, God can forgive anyone, and his grace covers a whole lot of sins. . . . And I thought, *Hey, that's pretty simple. Just tell God I'm sorry and move on.* But it wasn't as easy as it sounded.

My lies and sins were so entrenched with others, mainly Ryun and Sierra, that they couldn't be easily undone. Still, I kept praying, hoping my prayers would count for something. But it was Valentine's Day. And besides being bummed for missing the upcoming Little Lambs snow trip, I was sitting in my room, thinking about the evening that Ryun and Sierra would be enjoying at The Lantern. And, let me tell you, it was almost more than this girl could take!

So imagine my surprise when my mom told me that Sierra was on the phone. Especially since I'd been pretty much avoiding her and everyone else for the last couple of days. Not only that, but I'd told my family that I was *not* taking phone calls. They all knew about the board's inquiry and that I wasn't in a good mood. And so far everyone had taken me seriously. But somehow Sierra managed to work her way past my poor old mom tonight.

"She said it's an emergency," Mom told me.

I sighed in exasperation as I took the phone, waiting for her to leave before I spoke. "What *is* it, Sierra?" I finally asked.

"Kenzie," she began. "Carin told me what happened at your church. I think it's awful. I feel so bad for you."

"Do you?" I tried to keep my voice even. I wasn't completely sure Sierra wasn't involved in all this. Still, I wasn't ready to make any accusations.

"It's probably politics or something," she finally said in a it's-no-big-deal kind of way. "Don't let them get you down."

kenzie's story

215

Well, that just fried me. "Great advice, Sierra!"
I practically yelled. "Maybe it works in your perfect
little world. But out here things are tougher."

"Perfect world?" She sounded thoroughly insulted
now. "Hey, who's the one who spent weeks in the
hospital? And who walked out of that accident without a scratch?"

Now I really felt rotten. "Look, Sierra," I said in
a calmer tone, "I didn't mean to take it out on you.
It's just—it's not fair. I really love working with those
little kids. They expect me to be there for them."

"I know. That's why I called. I know life hasn't
been going that great for you."

"Tell me about it."

"But I—I need a favor."

"I'm not exactly in a good-deeds kind of mood,
Sierra."

"I wouldn't ask you if I had another choice. It's
not just for me. It's for Ryun."

"Ryun?" I glanced at the clock now. "Hey, aren't
you late for your big Valentine's date?"

"That's why I'm calling," she said. "I couldn't get
ahold of Ryun, and I'm feeling sick. My fever's back.
I can't go to the restaurant. And I can't reach Ryun
on his cell."

"So, call the restaurant." *Get a clue,* I thought.

"I tried. They're busy," Sierra said. "People must
be trying to get in. I hate to have to ask you this,
but I can't stand to think of Ryun just sitting there,
waiting for me. Besides, he's paid for that dinner
in advance. He should get to eat it. So I need you
to go there and take my place. Have dinner with

degrees of betrayal

Ryun. Please? I won't ever ask you for another thing. Do this one thing for me. Please, Kenzie?"

"You don't know what you're asking." I tried not to laugh at the irony, but I was thinking this was just too ridiculous. Why would she ask *me,* of all people, to do this? It made no sense.

"Please, Kenzie? Tell Ryun I'm not feeling good and that I begged you to come and have dinner with him. Do it for me? He doesn't deserve to spend the whole night waiting for me to show."

I couldn't believe this. Had Sierra lost her mind?

"Kenzie?"

"Oh, all right." I finally said. I hung up the phone and thought how whacked it was for me to go to The Lantern to tell Ryun that Sierra was standing him up, that she was sending me in her place. How stupid was that?

Then I thought about Ryun. I imagined him sitting there, wearing his best suit . . . all his so-called friends seated as couples at the tables around him. They would watch him, tossing suspicious glances his way, then snickering and gossiping. Suddenly I couldn't stand it. I refused to let Ryun go through something like that alone.

Ryun and I might both be a total mess, but, hey, at least we could be a mess together. I knew I was probably slitting my own throat as I put on the clingy black dress that Holly had picked out for me last summer. She'd said I looked like a million bucks in it. Then I picked out a pair of black strappy sandals that Sierra had insisted looked trampy, but I liked. Besides, I was on my own tonight. I hurried to

kenzie's story

apply a little makeup and finally slipped on the delicate pearl necklace around my neck. Perfect. I put on my coat and convinced my dad to drive me to my mystery dinner date.

"I didn't know you had a date," said Lark, an eyebrow arched with suspicion.

"I didn't either," I chirped. "Apparently Sierra had planned a surprise dinner for some of her friends at The Lantern."

My dad whistled. "The Lantern? That's pretty expensive."

"I know," I said. "Isn't that generous of her?"

I moved some of my dad's carpentry tools from the passenger seat of his pickup, then swept off the loose sawdust before I climbed in.

"Sorry about that," he said as he turned on the ignition. "Didn't know I was going to be chauffeuring a lovely princess tonight."

I laughed. "Don't worry, Dad. I'm nobody's princess."

He frowned as he headed toward town. "You're my princess."

27

It was a quarter to eight by the time my
dad dropped me off at The Lantern. I nearly tripped
over the curb as I leaped out the door, then hurried
into the restaurant. I hoped Ryun was still here. I
couldn't bear the idea of having to call up my dad
to come back here to pick me up. And for all I knew
this could be a big setup. Sierra might be sitting
with Ryun right now, just waiting for me to make
my big entrance so everyone could laugh at me.
I seriously considered turning back. Maybe my dad
was still outside.

"Coat, miss?" asked a man in a tuxedo by the
door. He was holding out his hands.

"Uh, yeah, I guess so." I slipped out of my coat,
then gave my hair a fluff. I started scanning the
room, then spotted Ryun standing near the entrance

of the restaurant, cell phone in one hand. I was
relieved. He appeared to be alone.

When our eyes met, I thought, *Okay, Ryun, this
is a test. This is only a test. Do you really care about
me or not? Let the games begin.*

So I smiled and began to walk toward him.
He looked surprised but smiled back. *One point for
you, Ryun.*

"Hey, sorry I'm late," I told him.

"You're not late." He smiled again, then peered
nervously over my shoulder. "Sierra's the one who's
late. So why are you here?"

"Sierra called," I said quietly, trying to be dis-
creet. "She said she's not feeling well. She asked me
if I'd sit in for her, because she knew you'd already
shelled out for the meal ahead of time."

"She did?" He looked really shocked and confused
now. No points for that.

"She did," I repeated. Then I smiled at him again.
"And I'm glad she couldn't come." I waited for a
response, but he didn't say anything. *Minus a point
for that, Ryun.* But I continued with the game. "I
wanted it to be *me* here with you tonight, Ryun.
So I'm glad."

I was well aware of the curious glances being
tossed our direction, and I could already see Carin's
brows lifted high, her lips moving furiously as
she told Mick, her new boyfriend, that I was here—
with Ryun. But I tried to block them out. I tried to
pretend that it was just Ryun and me, with the rest
of the world fading away for an evening.

But Ryun's eyes seemed troubled, like he was

struggling with the whole thing. I had to subtract more points. He was going into the hole now. *Is he wondering why Sierra didn't come—or regretting that I came instead? Is this all just a stupid mistake?* I considered turning around and leaving.

But in that same moment Ryun reached for my hand and said, "Let's go." Surprised, I had to give him a couple of points for this. Maybe even three. And then with my hand securely in his, he led me past our so-called friends and, gaining another point, pulled out a chair and seated me at a private corner table. *So he may be slow, but he's coming through.* He continued to hold my hand, as if he were telling all of them to go take a leap—that we were done with the game and were going to do as we pleased from here on out. Two more points.

Together we enjoyed an amazing evening. It was like everyone else totally disappeared. Oh, I knew that they were there. And I know they were probably all staring at us as we ate a really nice meal. I'm sure they were all talking about us as we lingered over dessert. And I suspected that someone, probably Carin, phoned Sierra. But I was glad. Maybe this game was finally coming to an end.

But then I'd been wrong before. Who knew? It might go into overtime.

Ryun and I were both feeling nervously happy as he drove me home. It was like we were both playing these parts now, acting like everything was okay, like everything that happened tonight was perfectly normal. He even walked me to the door

and kissed me. I imagined that this was the way
it would be from here on out. Ryun and I—walking
down the halls of High High together, holding
hands, and just letting everyone get over it.
Why not?

28

I was relieved. Ryun and I were finally out in the open. But I also knew we were both toast. All of our friends would probably disown us.

The first person who approached me was Holly, and her face didn't look happy. "Kenzie, what on earth got into you last night?"

"What do you mean?"

"What do you think I mean?"

"I only did what Sierra—"

"Sierra is brokenhearted, Kenzie. Devastated. She can't believe you pulled this sort of thing on her."

"Really?"

"That's all you can say? *Really?*"

"I don't see why she should be so surprised. I mean, she's the one who asked me to go have dinner with him—"

"That's not the story I heard."

I sighed. "And what *did* you hear, Holly?"

"I heard that Sierra had only wanted you to go tell Ryun that she couldn't make it last night, that she was really sick. She *thought* you were her best friend, Kenzie!" Holly looked really disgusted with me now.

"But that's not what Sierra told me—"

"What?" demanded Holly. "Are you trying to make me believe that Sierra actually told you to *go have dinner with her boyfriend?*"

"Believe what you want, Holly." Others were gathering around to listen now, but I wanted out of this conversation. I glanced over my shoulder, looking for Ryun and wondering what kind of treatment he was getting over this.

"You are too much, Kenzie," continued Holly. "What were you thinking?"

"I guess I wasn't thinking." I started to back away, but Holly wasn't done with me yet.

"To go to The Lantern, dressed like *that*, and after Sierra had asked you to let Ryun know that she couldn't make it." Holly sighed loudly. "Bad move, Kenzie."

"The only reason I stayed was because Sierra begged me to have dinner so that Ryun wouldn't feel bad—"

Holly's laughter cut me off. "Get real, Kenzie."

"She did," I pleaded, wanting her to believe me. "Sierra called me and begged me to go. She said she'd tried to call the restaurant and kept getting a busy signal and that she was sick and—"

"Yeah," said Carin, getting her two cents in. "That's what Sierra told me too. But that's all."

"That is *not* all." I stood up straighter. "Sierra told me to go have dinner with Ryun. She felt bad that he'd paid in advance and she couldn't go."

"Kenzie . . ." Carin sounded like she was talking to a four-year-old now. "Do you really expect anyone to believe *that?*"

I heard the others laughing and commenting now, tossing jabs and acting like I was a complete traitor. "No, I guess not," I said quietly. Not that anyone was listening. "I found it pretty hard to believe myself last night. But I fell for it."

"I'm sure," said Carin. "Like Sierra would really ask you, of all people, to go have dinner with her boyfriend on Valentine's Day. *Get real!*"

"Whatever."

"What you did last night really sucks, Kenzie," continued Carin. "It was low-down and cheap and slutty. And Sierra was completely shattered by it."

"Yeah, right."

"And if that's how you treat your friends," added Holly, "well, consider me *not* one of them."

"Me too," said Carin. As if she was ever my friend.

"Right." I turned and walked away, wishing that the floor in the hallway would open up and swallow me whole.

The only good thing about the rest of that awful day . . . for the rest of the week . . . was that no one even spoke to me. They avoided me like the plague. But I didn't really care. The charade was finally over.

And when Ryun and I wanted to talk or be together, we no longer had to sneak around and hide. Everything, well, almost everything, seemed to be out in the open now.

I felt bad for Sierra. But then she had brought a lot of this on herself. She was going around looking like the poor victim, but I was pretty sure that Valentine's Day had been a setup. Maybe we could all get on with our lives now. Or so I tried to make myself believe.

29

kenzie's story

Relieved that life seemed to be returning to
normal or something close, I felt that I should give
God a little bit of credit. So, since it was Sunday,
I decided I should at least go to church. I dragged
myself out of bed, showered, and dressed. I even
made it downstairs in time to go with my family
to church.

Unfortunately I had a headache, so it was hard
to concentrate on the sermon. But at least the music
was good. Finally it was over and we were walking
down the aisle to the door. That was when I noticed
Holly and Carin on the other side of the sanctuary.
It was obvious they were both looking at me, probably still talking about what a cheating slut I was
and how I had a lot of nerve to show my face in
church. Maybe they expected God to strike me

down with a lightning bolt or something equally spectacular.

Then I saw Carin turning to say something to her mom, and it suddenly hit me—*Carin's mom is on the Little Lambs board.* I paused in the aisle to stare at both of them, and they both looked at me as if I were a walking talking piece of garbage. Like they were thinking someone should take out the trash. That was when I knew—it was Carin who had told the lies about me.

But church wasn't the place for the kind of confrontation I would like to stage. And so I continued on outside to wait for my family. I sat down on the cement steps and put my head down on my knees.

"Kenzie?"

I looked to see Anna standing in front of me. "Are you okay?"

I shrugged. "I've been better." I felt really tired, and my head was throbbing.

"Want to talk?"

I considered this. I really would like to talk to someone who didn't think I was the devil. "Yeah, I kind of would."

"Want me to give you a ride home?" she offered. "We could grab a bite."

I forced a smile to my face. "Yeah, that'd be cool. Let me tell my parents."

The next thing I knew I was sitting in Anna's little car, telling her about the stupid Valentine's Day fiasco and how everyone hated me now.

"That sounds pretty typical," she said as she

pulled into a drive-in. We had decided it would be better to just sit in the car to eat.

"I guess." Then I told her about how I was being investigated by the Little Lambs board and how I was now certain that Carin was the mastermind behind it.

"But why?" asked Anna after we placed our orders.

"It might have to do with Sierra. Maybe it was Carin's way of getting back at me after the photo thing."

"Man, Kenzie," said Anna. "That's tough."

Our food arrived, but I wasn't very hungry. I could only drink some of my milk shake.

"You've really been through the wringer this year," she told me, like I wasn't already aware of that.

I nodded. "But that's not even the worst of it, Anna." I turned to look at her, wondering if I could really trust her.

"You're kidding?" She studied me. "There's more?"

"Oh yeah."

Her eyes grew wide. "Oh no, Kenzie. Don't tell me you're pregnant or have AIDS or are wanted for murder or something."

I sighed. "Well, it's not *that* bad. Can I totally trust you with this, Anna?"

"Kenzie, up until recently we've been best friends for, like, how long?"

"A long time." I shook my head. "And if I hadn't been such a moron, we'd still be best friends, right?"

"I guess you could say that." Anna sighed. "But the truth is, I wasn't such a great friend to you either, Kenzie."

"What do you mean?" I tried to remember when Anna ever did anything wrong.

"Well, I guess I was jealous of your new friends," she said. "And I probably said some things that weren't very nice."

"But you might've been right," I added.

"But I was judging them." She gave me a half smile. "And you too, I guess."

"Still, you were right, Anna. I think you were right about all of us."

"Well, it doesn't make me feel any better," she admitted. "Now, what did you want to tell me about?"

I closed my eyes and leaned back into the seat. "It's such a long, messed-up story, Anna. Are you sure you want—?"

"You can trust me, Kenzie," she said suddenly. "Honestly, as God is my witness, I won't repeat anything you say to anyone."

I opened my eyes and stared at her. I just *knew* she was telling the truth. And suddenly there was nothing quite as wonderful as the truth. I wished I had never turned my back on it in the first place. And so I told her what really happened the night of the wreck and how Ryun and I decided to just go with the police's assumption of who was driving that night.

"Wow." She just shook her head after I was finished. "That's unbelievable." Then she eyed me. "But what if Sierra gets her memory back, Kenzie? She'd totally blow this thing sky-high."

"I think she's already got her memory back, Anna."

"You're kidding!"

"I can't really say why—it's just a feeling. I think she knows, and I think she's trying to get back at us. In fact, I wonder if she doesn't have something to do with me losing my job at Little Lambs."

"Well, she and Carin are pretty close."

I nodded.

"And it makes sense that she'd be pretty mad at you for moving in on her boyfriend."

"I know."

"What a mess." Anna put what was left of our lunch on the tray outside her window. "It's hard to believe you could've gotten into something like this, Kenzie. I used to think you were one of the most grounded girls in the whole school. And now this."

"Yeah, it's pretty stupid. Believe me, I'm not proud."

"Are you feeling okay, Kenzie?" Anna was really studying me now.

"Huh?"

"You look kind of funny."

"Funny?" I frowned. "What do you mean?"

"Kind of splotchy. Here." She reached over and pulled down the visor in front of me to reveal a mirror.

I adjusted the mirror, then peered at my reflection. "Oh, my word!" I put my hands to my face in horror.

"Do you think you're having some kind of an allergic reaction?" she asked.

"I don't know. I've had this gruesome headache and my face feels all hot."

"We better get you home."

Blessing or curse? I asked myself as my
mom tucked me into bed in the middle of the day.
As it turned out I had the measles. The blessing was
that I wouldn't have to go to school for a while. The
curse was that I looked like something out of a bad
health class film and it was only going to get worse.

"Measles?" I said to my mom after she had made
her diagnosis. "How can I possibly have the measles?"

"I've heard it's going around, honey," she told me.

"But I don't know *anyone* who has the measles,"
I said.

"Well, you must've been around someone who
did. It must've been about a week ago. If you had
been at Little Lambs, I'd wonder if you got it there,
although I don't know of any children who've come
down with—"

"That's it," I told her. "I held this little boy at the hospital and he seemed to be kind of sick and he had a rash on his arms. But I didn't think—"

"That's probably it, honey. Measles are highly contagious."

"Yikes," said Lark, who had been sitting at the breakfast bar just staring at my face. "I'm getting out of here."

"Ugh, me too," yelled Josh.

"Measles!" said Aaron. "Red alert! Red alert!"

"Don't worry," my mom assured the three of them. "You can't get it."

"Why not?" I demanded.

"They've been immunized."

"They've been immunized?" I stared at my mom. "What about me?"

"Well . . ." She looked rather sheepish as she handed me some of her miracle vitamins. "When you were a baby, I was still in my anti-immunization era."

"It figures."

She handed me a tall glass of apple juice now. "Take those vitamins, honey. They might help."

"Did I get *any* immunizations?" I asked weakly.

"Of course." She put her cool hand on my fore-head now. "You had to have all the required ones. But measles was optional."

"And now I have the measles."

"Sorry, honey." She took my hand and pulled me to my feet. "And now we're getting you to bed." I felt powerless to resist as she led me upstairs and helped me into bed.

I watched as my mom closed my curtains. "The light's not good for your eyes, honey."

"How do you know all these things?" I asked.

"I'm a mom," she quipped. "It's just part of my job."

"Oh."

"Anything else I can get for you?"

I didn't feel like I wanted anything just now . . . well, other than for someone to put me out of my misery. "No," I said. "Except—I don't want to take any phone calls, Mom. I don't really want to talk to anyone."

"Not a problem."

"Except for maybe Anna," I said.

She smiled. "I'm glad that you and Anna are friends again."

I sighed. "So am I."

"Rest well."

"Thanks," I muttered as I leaned back and closed my eyes.

Then she tiptoed away and I was left with just me and my spots.

■   ■   ■

The week slowly passed, and I managed to survive. My whole family really treated me nicely. Part of me felt like I could just stay like this forever. Maybe that's how Sierra felt when she was in the hospital— everyone waited on you and acted like you're the princess. Plus, my mom made some really delicious soups. So it wasn't bad, not really.

Not only that, but my phone calls were fielded by my family members, mostly Lark, who developed an answer that sounded almost like a recording. "No, Kenzie *cannot* come to the phone right now. She is sick in bed with the measles and she cannot be disturbed." I almost wanted to laugh every time I heard her saying it—which I had to admit was less and less. No one seemed to be calling me anymore. Well, other than Ryun—and Anna. Anna had been by to visit me several times and even picked up homework for me so I didn't fall behind.

"And the gossip is finally starting to die down," she assured me on Thursday.

"*You* hear gossip?"

"Good grief, Kenzie, I'm not deaf."

"Sorry," I told her.

"Anyway, here's what's going on. First of all, everyone still feels very sorry for Sierra. It's like her little band of friends won't leave her side these days. Like they're protecting her from the *evil Ryun.*" She laughed. "I'm sure they'd be protecting her from you too, if you were there."

I sighed, thankful that I wasn't. "How's Ryun holding up?" I finally asked, almost afraid to hear the answer. I felt guilty and worried, sure that I'd hurt him badly by not taking his calls. But I just wasn't ready to talk to him yet. I was too confused, especially after telling the whole story to Anna. I knew I had to come clean with it, but I wasn't sure how. Or when. So I didn't trust myself to talk to him or see him for the time being. I needed time to sort this thing out.

"I haven't really seen too much of Ryun," continued Anna. "I noticed he was in the workout room one day when I had to take a form down to the PE department. It looked like he was pretty focused. I guess he's getting ready to play soccer again."

"That's a relief," I said. And I *was* relieved. But I guess I was a little ticked too. I wanted him to suffer for all our stupidity—just a little. I mean, it seemed like *I'd* been the one paying for our mistakes. Why should he get off so easily?

It was good to have this week to stay at home, mostly in bed, and think about these things. Sort of like a pot that's been set on the back burner and allowed to simmer for a while. I had time to slow down, to examine my life, and to actually pray without distractions.

Of course, all good things always come to an end, and by the following weekend I had no more excuses to lie around in bed and be waited on. The last traces of my spots had faded to nothing more than a memory, and my mom said I didn't have such a bad case of measles. And *now* she told me I could've been scarred for life.

I didn't tell her I already *was* scarred for life.

kenzie's story

31

Anna gave me a ride to school on Monday, and I was so thankful to have her by my side as I walked onto campus. I wasn't sure what I thought my ex-friends might do to me—burn me at the stake, stone me, or simply freeze me out.

Once again I tried to keep a low profile, but it was impossible not to see the looks I was getting, hear the whispered innuendos, feel the hostile glances that quickly turned away, as if I weren't even worth looking at. I guess I should have been thankful, though. Their reaction to me had probably softened with the passing of time.

And although their looks and jabs hurt—I couldn't deny that—it was also something of a relief. Like being able to get off a wild carnival ride that just kept going and going, even if you're sick and dizzy and ready to hurl.

■ ■ ■

I actually survived my first week back at school. Now I was standing outside in the cold breeze, trying to avoid looks that were even chillier. But Anna and I had been meeting out here all week. I couldn't complain that she was a little late since it was really nice of her to take me home during lunch hour, even though she still had two more classes. Of course, Anna didn't have to take that many classes to graduate, but she was taking honors classes. Like I'd be doing if I hadn't given up my afternoons to work at Little Lambs, which, of course, I was no longer doing. But I tried not to think about that as I pulled my sweatshirt sleeves down over my hands to keep my fingers warm.

"Kenzie?"

I knew that voice without even looking. I knew it was Ryun and that there was no place to run. I was still confused, so I'd avoided him all week, even though he'd tried to talk to me.

"Can we talk?"

I looked past him to see if Anna was anywhere close by. I wished she'd burst out the doors right now and I could say, "Sorry, I've got to go." But she didn't appear.

"Kenzie, we really need to talk," he said again.

I nodded. "I know."

"What's going on?"

I was determined not to give in to the pressure I felt just being close to him. "Nothing," I answered, adjusting my backpack and looking toward the door. I was stalling for time. "I'm just waiting for Anna."

"I mean, what's going on with you, Kenzie? Why are you doing this to me?"

"Doing what?"

"Brushing me off. Why? After all I've given up for you, why are you doing this to me?"

"All *you've* given up?" I repeated.

"I broke up with Sierra for you, Kenzie."

"I don't know, Ryun." I was finally ready to admit what I'd been feeling inside. "I actually think *Sierra* broke up with you. And it might've looked like you guys were still together, but I think she broke up with you when she got her memory back."

"Sierra hasn't got her memory back," he insisted.

"I think she does."

"How do you know?"

"I just have this feeling, Ryun."

He shook his head. "That's crazy, Kenzie. Sierra's memory hasn't come back. She's never said a word about it to me or anyone."

"Maybe she doesn't want anyone to know."

"I think you may be losing it, Kenzie." He tapped his finger to his head now like I was nuts. "Maybe having the measles has affected your mind."

"Thanks," I told him.

"Hey, I'm sorry," he said in a softer voice. "It's just that I don't think Sierra has her memory back."

"But what if she did?"

He shrugged. "She won't, Kenzie. And if she does, like I said, we'll deal with it."

"But what if I told her the truth?" I asked.

"Why would you want to do that?" he asked, looking puzzled. "Why now, after all this time?"

"The truth has to come out eventually."

"What do you mean?"

"I mean, I'm ready for it to come out now."

There was a long pause, and then he said, "Please, Kenzie. Please don't ruin this for me. My knee is just getting better and I've got the scholarship from Duke—you know it'll all fall apart."

"But I can't keep living the lie, Ryun. It's wrong. And I can't handle the pressure anymore."

"Just give me some time," he pleaded with me. "Just a little time to figure things out. *Please!*"

I knew Ryun had much more at stake than I did. Since I'd let it go for so long, I figured a little more time couldn't do any more damage. "Okay," I finally agreed. "But we have to tell Sierra everything."

"Yes, but not today."

"But soon," I told him. "I can only promise you that I won't say anything until Monday. Is that okay?"

"Thanks, Kenzie," he said. "I knew you had a heart." He looked into my eyes now. "Just follow your heart and everything will be fine."

We hugged for a while and finally I stepped back. "I better go," I told him.

"Don't you need a ride?"

"Anna's giving me one," I explained, glancing over my shoulder.

"Want to go out tonight?" he asked, looking sincere and hopeful. "Or sometime this weekend?"

"Maybe," I said. "Why don't you call me later?"

"Yeah, okay." He smiled and I felt that old warm rush running through me. "I was just on my way to the gym to work out in the weight room."

"How's the knee?" I asked, realizing I hadn't asked him that for a while.

"Pretty good," he said. "Almost like new."

"I'm glad."

I spied Anna now. She was hanging over by one of the big columns next to the front entrance, only about 10 feet away. I suspected that she was listening, but I didn't really mind.

He hugged me again. "I'll call." And he turned and walked slowly away.

He was barely gone when Anna came over to join me. "Everything okay?" she asked.

"Were you listening?"

She smiled sheepishly. "Sorry. I'd just come out the door when you guys were in the thick of it. I didn't want to interrupt, but there was no way to escape without being seen. Besides, I figured I could be on guard for you, in case anyone else popped in for the show, you know."

"Thanks," I told her.

We talked about my conversation with Ryun as she drove me home. "Why more time?" she asked as she turned down my street. "You guys have had months to tell the truth."

"I'm so ready to be done with this," I admitted. "And I don't even care that I'm going to take some heat. But I feel guilty about Ryun. I mean, he's got everything at stake. Maybe the right thing to do is to give him a little more time to work things out."

I could tell Anna wasn't convinced. "Why don't you pray about it, Kenzie?"

I considered this. "Okay, I'll do that."

"Hang in there."

I got out of the car, waved at her, and went into the house. And then I went straight up into my room, closed the door, and got on my knees and prayed. I knew I had to tell the truth, but I was worried about what it would do to Ryun. He really was the one who had the most to lose.

"Well, today's the big day, right?"

Anna said the following Monday as we walked into school. I'd already told her about my plan to come clean today.

"Yeah," I said. "I can hardly believe it's all going to be out in the open before long."

"You're going to feel lots better," she said.

"Well, eventually. I think it's going to take a while."

My heart was racing and my palms were clammy. I wasn't even sure I could do this thing. But I knew that I had to tell Sierra the truth. Just get it out. And my plan was to catch up with her after second period—econ. But I was really scared that I'd get cold feet.

And then I couldn't find Sierra. Not in class. Not in the halls or the cafeteria. Not anywhere.

When I got home I called her on her cell, but she wasn't answering. She'd even turned the messaging off. When I called her home phone, I was told by Mrs. Reynolds in a very crisp voice that my calls were no longer welcome in their home.

Even so, I decided to try again later, hoping that her parents might be gone since I knew they went out a lot. Only that time I got Jack, who informed me that Sierra had no interest in talking to me and that I shouldn't keep calling their house. "Did you know we could have a restraining order put on you?" Jack finally told me in a fairly hostile voice.

"Please, Jack, can't you just tell her I need to talk?" I pleaded. "It's *really* important."

Before she hung up, Jack said she would relay my message.

Still determined to tell Sierra the truth, I sat down and wrote a three-page letter—a complete confession that could, I felt sure, be used against me in a court of law. At the end I told her that I was sorry, for like the umpteenth time, and then I asked her to forgive me. But even as I wrote those words I knew the forgiveness part was a long shot and that I didn't deserve it anyway. But it was worth a try. I planned to hand deliver the letter to her tomorrow.

■ ■ ■

Sierra was in school on Tuesday, but as usual, she was totally ignoring me. Then she was called out of class during English lit. And the next time I saw her, she seemed a little upset. But I was determined as I walked up to her. I was going to get this thing done. I held out my letter and said, "We need to talk."

But she simply looked straight through me, as if I weren't there, and then she just walked away.

Well, fine, I thought. *I can't force her to talk to me. But she's got to read this letter. I have to let her know what really happened that night.*

Then I reminded myself that maybe she *already* knew. But then why wouldn't she just come out and say something? Was she just trying to torture us?

And, obviously, she had the power to torture us. We'd handed it over to her when we first began betraying her. And we'd given her even more ways since then. She could torture Ryun because of his scholarship and everything he had to lose. And she could torture me by ignoring me and, even more, by refusing to forgive me. Sierra, as always, had all the power.

Later on in the day, I was called down to the principal's office. I expected the worst. And when I saw Ryun also waiting outside, I knew that the time had come. The jig was up. I glanced around the office, certain that the police had to be here somewhere. And sure enough, there were two uniformed officers standing in Principal Waters' office. The three of them were talking. I looked at Ryun, and I could tell he was just as nervous. I felt certain that we'd soon be hauled down to city hall, questioned, booked, and possibly jailed. I wondered if the police would cuff us right here at school. Would our classmates watch as we were read our rights and shoved

into the back of a patrol car? I wanted to tell Ryun
that it wasn't me, that I hadn't even had a chance
to talk to Sierra yet, but before I could say a word,
Principal Waters told us to come into his office.

"Do you remember Sergeant McCarthy?" he
asked.

I shook my head.

"I do," said Ryun solemnly. "From the accident."

"That's right," said McCarthy, but he was holding
out his hand and smiling now. Ryun extended his
hand and the two of them shook. The next thing
I knew McCarthy was shaking my hand too. Pretty
weird.

"Sit down," said Principal Waters. "We have
something to tell you."

And suddenly they were talking about an
upcoming assembly that was scheduled for Thursday. Naturally, I had absolutely no idea what this
had to do with us. Was I hallucinating? Maybe
I'd fainted from fear and was just dreaming this.

"We thought about surprising you," said
McCarthy. "But then we decided that might not
be very nice."

I still wasn't totally following this, but I tried
to act like I knew what they were talking about as
they explained how even the middle-school kids
were invited to attend this special assembly. Were
they planning on arresting Ryun and me in front of
the whole high school and middle school? Making
us into shameful examples of what we don't want
our kids growing up to be? And, great, Lark would
be there and have the privilege of watching her older

sister being cuffed in front of thousands. She'd be so proud.

"I don't quite understand," Ryun said finally. I was relieved that one of us could still speak. "Are you saying that you're giving us an award?"

McCarthy laughed now. "I thought you'd already heard about it. Didn't your friend Sierra tell you?"

We both shook our heads like dummies. *Crash dummies,* I was thinking.

"Well, it's the mayor's award. For when you saved your friend's life last fall by pulling her from the burning car. The mayor thought it was about time to honor you two."

Now Ryun was smiling and nodding, like this was no big surprise.

But I was still in a state of shock. "And Sierra knows about this?" I finally managed to ask.

"Yes, we've already spoken to her," said our principal. "She's even going to give a little speech."

I nodded again. I could just imagine what she might say. And then we were excused. My knees felt like warm Jell-O as Ryun and I stepped out into the empty hallway.

"See," said Ryun, sounding satisfied. "Just like I told you. Everything's going to be fine."

"No," I said. "Everything is not. Sierra knows the truth. And I'm guessing she plans to make complete fools of us at the assembly this Thursday."

Then, without waiting for his response, I hurried down the hall to take refuge in the girls' john. I had so wanted this to be over with—and today. But now we had this ridiculous awards assembly. Honestly, I didn't know if I could live through it. I leaned over the sink and splashed cold water on my face. I wanted out of this whole mess. Maybe I could just be sick that day. I decided to search for Anna. Maybe she'd have something encouraging to say.

When I found her and told her what was happening, Anna couldn't believe it. "But I thought you told Sierra the truth," she said.

"I tried to," I told her. "But she wouldn't take the letter."

"Maybe you should just talk to her," said Anna. "Tell her face-to-face."

"How can I tell it to her face-to-face if she won't even listen to me for more than five seconds?"

"I don't know." We discussed it some more during art, but neither of us really knew what the answer was, short of Anna pinning Sierra down while I told her. And I had a feeling that wouldn't go over too well.

It was sunny as we left school, but I felt like a gray cloud was still following me around. I was sure it wouldn't go away until this Sierra thing was wrapped up.

Then, as if I didn't have enough trouble, my mom had told me that morning that the Little Lambs board had requested I make another trip to the hospital lab today. "It's a spur-of-the-moment drug test," she apologized, "to help establish your innocence."

Even though I knew it was a ridiculous waste of time, I also knew that if I passed the test, which I certainly would, I'd be allowed to return to my job.

And as much as I hated going to the stupid hospital lab, I did want my job back. And so I went.

Fortunately Nurse Sourpuss wasn't there. And because I already had on lightweight clothes, no one made me strip down. The whole thing was actually quite painless, and I kept telling myself, *This* will *get me my job back*.

33

I had hoped to give Sierra my letter the following day, but she wasn't at school. Then I overheard Holly and Carin talking about how Sierra's roommate from the hospital had died. I remembered seeing this extremely old woman and I knew that Sierra had been close to her, but I was surprised that Sierra was taking it so hard. Carin said she was so upset that she couldn't even come to school. I felt bad for Sierra, and it made me want to talk to her even more. But, just like before, her cell phone was turned off and her family was screening her calls. I actually considered making an appearance at her house but was worried that someone (like her little sister) might even call the police.

I seriously considered skipping school on Thursday.

But I knew that would be the chicken way out. Besides, I told myself, *Why not just get this whole thing over with in a really big way? If I'm going down, why not do it with flair. Right?*

And I figured Sierra had to show up for the assembly. Maybe I could give her my letter during first period, right there in class with everyone watching so she couldn't throw it back in my face. At least I'd know she had it. What she did with it after that would be up to her.

To my relief, Sierra did make an appearance in English lit. Of course, she was nearly 15 minutes late, but Ms. Rowe completely ignored that as Sierra took her seat. I eyed her off and on through-out class. She looked so upset that I wasn't sure if I should really follow through with my plan. But as soon as the bell rang, I got up and hurried over to Sierra. And I could tell by her eyes that she'd been crying.

"Sierra, I'm really sorry," I said quietly. "About Missouri, I mean. I just heard the news. And she seemed like a nice lady."

Sierra looked at me. It was the first time she'd really looked at me since Valentine's Day, and I could tell I finally had her attention. "She was amazing," was all she said.

Finally I turned and walked away. I knew I'd blown my last chance to give her the letter just now. But somehow the timing seemed all wrong. I just hoped I'd get another chance before the awards assembly. More than anything I wanted her to know the truth. I wanted to come clean.

As it turned out, everyone was released early from classes, and as far as I could tell, Sierra was nowhere in sight. I spied a few kids slipping out the back doors, using this opportunity to escape from school early. And I didn't blame them. Part of me would have loved to skip the whole thing too. But a bigger part said, *Let's do this thing! Just get it over with.*

Anna went with me to the gym. Then the principal saw me and directed me to go up and sit onstage. Feeling like I was preparing for my execution, I sat down in a folding metal chair and waited. Ryun came in a few minutes later and immediately started joking around with the principal and the mayor. Like he didn't have a care in the world.

I just sat there silently, staring down at my hands in my lap and thinking that all I wanted was to get this thing over and done with. Whether I left in the back of a squad car or with Anna made little difference anymore. I just wanted it over, once and for all, finished.

Principal Waters, the mayor, and one of the police officers spoke to the crowd, but I didn't pay any attention to their words. I only wanted to hear what Sierra had to say. Then it was time to receive our awards, and Ryun and I both took turns shaking the mayor's hand. Feeling like a complete hypocrite, I took my stupid plaque (which I planned to burn as soon as I got home) and waited.

Now it was Sierra's turn to stand at the podium.

I had to admit she looked a little worse for wear. Not her usual image of perfection.

It also seemed obvious, at least to me, that she'd been crying. But she still managed to present herself with grace and decorum. Even so, I braced myself for her scathing words . . . preparing myself for the audience's stunned and outraged response. I wondered what the mayor would say. And would Sergeant McCarthy call down to city hall for backup?

The gym grew surprisingly quiet as the microphone buzzed loudly and we all waited for Sierra to say something. But it was like she was frozen or stuck. Then Principal Waters said, "Now!" To his embarrassment, his voice was amplified across the gym, and the silence was broken with ripples of laughter.

That's when Sierra finally began to speak. I wasn't sure if I could bear to listen, but I knew I had to try. My heart was pounding so loudly that I actually missed her opening words, but I forced myself to focus when I heard the word *accident*.

". . . since that accident, to all of us—Kenzie, Ryun, and me," she said in a conversational tone, not exactly like a speech. "Not everything has been easy. Or good." She paused and the gym grew quiet again.

I thought, *Okay, now it's coming. She's going to tell everyone what really happened that night.*

"Memory's a funny thing," she continued. "There's a lot I want to forget about that accident. And a lot I want to remember. Someone really wise once told me that life is about remembering the right things and forgetting the wrong."

Now she turned and looked at Ryun and me. I looked right back at her, trying to communicate with my eyes, saying, *Go ahead, Sierra, just get it over with. I'm ready to face the music now.*

"There are a lot of things I'm going to try to forget," she said slowly, meaningfully. "But I want to remember that you pulled me out of the car. Thank you."

And that was it—her speech was over. The audience clapped.

I should have been relieved. I should have been thankful that Sierra didn't blow the horn on us. But instead I was angry, like I almost wished she had. *Am I going totally crazy?* It didn't help, either, that Ryun was smiling at me—like we we were home free and invincible now. I wanted to grab the microphone and tell everyone to stop. I wanted to say, "Wait a minute, that's *not* how it was. Don't you want to hear the real story?"

But I didn't.

Principal Waters and the mayor left the stage. But a wild rush of emotions flooded me just then. I know I should've been relieved. I should've been willing to simply turn and walk away, forgetting this whole ugly thing. But somehow it all became clear to me in that moment. Somehow I knew that Sierra wasn't as much of a victim as she'd pretended to be. Suddenly a lot of things seemed to make perfect sense.

I turned to Sierra, actually blocking the stairs so she couldn't escape me this time. "You *know!*" I said in a voice so intense it surprised even me.

Sierra just looked shocked . . . and maybe a little confused.

"You haven't lost your memory," I continued. "You've known all along about the accident! I don't know what kind of game you're playing, Sierra. But I'm tired of playing it with you."

She stared at me now, as if trying to see who I really was. "I'm tired too, Kenzie. But I'm done. I don't want to play anymore."

I continued to stare at her, longing for her to come clean too. "It *was* you, wasn't it, Sierra?" I demanded. "You and Carin? Right? You're the ones who got me fired from Little Lambs."

She nodded, but not in a pleased or proud way. "It was. I'm sorry, Kenzie." And she actually seemed sincere. "I was just so mad at you for letting me take the blame and—"

"What was I supposed to do?" I said loudly. "I didn't lie. The police just assumed you were driving. And Ryun let them. He was driving without a license—"

"Why?" She seemed truly surprised.

"His license was suspended."

Sierra looked stunned now, like she had no idea.

"What are you going to do now?" I demanded.

"I don't know," Sierra said slowly. "But I think you should talk to Sergeant McCarthy."

"Then why wouldn't you talk to me?" I demanded. "I've been trying to tell you the truth for days." I pulled my rumpled letter from my pocket and held it out to her. "I've been trying to give you this. I wanted you to know what really happened. But you wouldn't let me."

"No," Sierra said sadly. "But I think everything will come out eventually."

Just then Ryun appeared. "Everything all right?"

We both turned to look at him. It was amazing

how confident he seemed. Like he'd just scored the winning goal. Our hero.

"Everything is *not* okay," I told him. "Sierra has had her memory back for some time."

"No way." Ryun laughed, but he looked uneasy. "She couldn't have faked that."

"I did lose my memory," Sierra admitted. "At least at first. But I got it back in the hospital."

Ryun looked stunned. "Then why—?" But he stopped himself, as if a realization was kicking in. "What are you going to do now? Have you told the police?"

I just stared at Ryun—the guy I thought I was in love with. The guy Sierra had thought she was in love with. And I wondered—did he even care about us? About all the suffering we'd gone through? Or did he just care about whether he was going to get caught or not? Who was this guy, anyway?

"I could have told the whole town today, Ryun— police, students, parents, newspaper, everybody." Sierra was speaking in a calm voice. "And I didn't. I'm not even sure why I didn't. But, no, I'm not going to the police."

Ryun relaxed, like everything was going to be okay again.

"But you need to know that all I've thought about since I got my memory back has been revenge. I wanted to get even." Sierra had a little spark in her eye now. "I've done some things, Ryun, some things I can't undo. I wanted to hurt you." She stared right at him now. "I've talked to Duke. I told them about your leg."

Ryun actually laughed. "You did not. I don't believe you. *They* wouldn't believe you, even if you *did* tell them." He put his arm around me. "You know what?" he said. "I'm not buying into any of this."

"Ryun." Sierra paused and looked straight at him. "I'm sorry. Be careful." And then she just walked away.

"Do you think?" Ryun looked at me now, his eyes pleading, almost as if he expected there was some way I could make this thing right for him. "Do you think she really did that?"

"I'm sure of it," I told him. And then I walked away.

■　　■　　■

Later that day I felt bad for just walking out on Ryun without talking it out, so I tried to call him. I called his cell over and over again, but I couldn't reach him.

That same night, when my brothers were at
Scouts, I told my parents I had something important
to tell them. Naturally Lark was all ears, and I figured it wouldn't hurt for her to hear my confession
as well. She already knew a lot about my life anyway. Besides, maybe she'd learn something from my
stupidity.

"This isn't going to be easy to tell you," I began
after they were all seated in the family room.
"I guess I'll just start off by saying I'm sorry."

I could tell by my parents' faces that they were
nervous. But Lark seemed almost amused, like she
couldn't wait to see how I'd blown it this time.

"Last fall when we got into the car wreck, I told
a lie." I took in a breath and continued. "I did it to
protect Ryun. He had been driving Sierra's car that

night when the wreck happened. Sierra had been driving earlier, but she'd been driving crazy. . . ." I tried to remember what was going on that night. I mean, what was *really* going on. I'd lied about it so much that the truth felt kind of foggy and blurry.

"Why was she driving crazy?" asked my mom.

I forced the words out. "It was my fault."

"But you weren't driving, were you?" asked my dad.

"No, but it was my fault she was acting crazy."

"Had you kids been drinking?" my dad put in suddenly.

"No, it wasn't like that. If you quit asking questions, I'll just tell you." They nodded and I continued. Lark was leaning forward now, eyes open wide, like she was watching some great scene in a movie or sneaking some MTV when she thought no one was looking.

"Remember when I went to Virginia last summer to visit the university?"

They nodded.

"Well, I ran into Ryun Lee there. Actually we were paired together for the evening. And we just hit it off, you know. It became pretty clear that we really liked each other."

"Well, you do seem to be good friends, honey," offered my mom.

I knew that she liked Ryun, but her comments weren't helping. "Yeah, well, it was more than *that*, Mom." I sighed. "This isn't easy, you know."

"Sorry, I'll keep quiet."

"So anyway, I thought maybe he was going to break up with Sierra, but he didn't. And then Sierra and I were becoming better friends, but I continued to see Ryun too. It just got a little messy. I kept thinking it would work out, that Ryun would break up with Sierra, but it just kept going . . ."

"A love triangle," said Lark dramatically.

I rolled my eyes. "Yeah, whatever. Anyway, it all hit the fan at the game. Sierra found out, and she was getting all crazy about it in the car."

"When she was driving?" asked my dad.

I nodded. "And so Ryun took over driving, even though he had a suspended license. When Ryun was driving like 60 miles an hour, she opened the door and was going to jump out.

"So I was holding on to her and screaming and Ryun was trying to help. The next thing we know, we're all over the road, then rolling."

My words were pouring out. I was hoping my mom wouldn't interrupt.

"Was it true that you kids pulled Sierra from the burning car?" asked my dad.

"Yes. That's true."

"Then you did save her life," said my dad.

"I guess. But Ryun's driving also endangered her life."

"That's true. But if she hadn't tried to jump—" put in my dad.

"Yeah. The thing is, I let the police believe Sierra was the driver. I didn't lie to them, but I didn't correct the story either. I guess I felt sorry for Ryun because telling the police that he was driving could have messed up his life. And I guess I was in love with him."

"Meaning you're *not* in love with him now?" demanded Lark, as if she worked for the DA's office.

I said it slowly, trying to believe it myself. "I was. But I'm not anymore. Too much has happened to make it work."

"That's a relief," said my dad.

"Anyway, I want everyone to know the truth now. And I wanted to start with you guys."

"Thank you, honey," said my mom.

Then I went on to tell them about all the complications this had caused for me. Even how I thought it was why a complaint was made against me to Little Lambs.

"Well, that's not right." My dad frowned. "Maybe someone should look into whoever it was who filed the complaint."

"Or maybe it's what I deserve." I began to cry. Both my parents got up then and put their arms around me. Even Lark joined the huddle.

"Well, you're telling the truth now," my mom said. "That's the best you can do at the moment."

"And I'm going to find a way to talk to Sierra," I told them. "I already told Ryun we had to tell the police the truth."

"It's a mess, isn't it?" said my mom.

"Tell me about it," I said. "I guess you'll want to punish me."

My parents eyed each other, as if they were considering an appropriate punishment. I was thinking grounding, housework, doing all the laundry until I was 18.

"I don't really see why *we* should punish you," my dad finally said. My mom was nodding. "Seems that you've been doing a pretty good job of that yourself."

■　■　■

I felt a little bit better after coming clean with my family. The old quote is right—There *is* something healing about telling the truth. But I also needed to tell the whole truth to Sergeant McCarthy too.

So that same evening I called up Sergeant McCarthy. I told him I had a confession to make about the accident. I didn't mention Ryun's involvement yet. I just said I wanted to change some things on my statement. To say he sounded a little shocked is an understatement. Then he scheduled an appointment for me to come down and talk to him first thing tomorrow morning on Friday. I wished he would've just let me come today. But I also understood . . . the man must have a life. He probably just wanted to go home and have dinner with his wife and kids. He probably wanted to call it a day too. Even so, I tossed and turned in my bed all night. I prepared myself for the worst.

■　■　■

Early the next morning my dad drove me down to city hall, where I made a complete statement. I felt

pretty sure McCarthy was going to book me now—
take my photo and fingerprints and maybe even
lock me up since I was nearly 18. But to my surprise,
he just let me go.

"Didn't I break some kind of law?" I asked him.

"You lied in your previous statement," he told me
in a serious voice. "And there could be consequences
later on. But because you've come forward and been
honest with us now, I seriously doubt that you'll be
prosecuted." He cleared his throat. "I can't say the
same for your friend Ryun."

I felt a mixture of humiliation and relief as we
left the station. My dad told me that I'd handled
it well, but I was numb as we drove home. I felt
bad for Ryun. I didn't really want to see him get
into serious trouble. I felt sorry for him. Sorry and
confused.

But my feelings didn't change what I knew I had
to do. And it wouldn't be easy. I finally reached
Ryun via cell and asked him to meet me at the park.
But the earliest he could meet was the next day, Sat-
urday. Then I called Anna and told her I needed her
to back me up. She promised to drive me there and
to hang out at the park until I was done.

■ ■ ■

"What about us?" Ryun said the next day, still looking slightly stunned.

We'd taken a walk in the park, and I'd decided
that I might as well say what I'd come to say right
off the bat.

"Us?" I studied him for a moment, then sighed. "There is no *us*, Ryun. Not anymore."

"But what about–?"

"We might've had something," I told him, "but we did it all wrong. We broke the rules, we cheated, we lied . . . and we hurt Sierra. And even though that's behind us now . . ." I shook my head, wondering if that was even true. Would it ever be behind us? "Well, I just don't think we could start over."

"But what if–?" He seemed desperate now, almost pleading.

"And even if we could," I continued, wanting this to be over with as quickly as possible, "I don't think I'd want to, Ryun. I'm not that same girl anymore. I don't even want to be."

"But, Kenzie–"

"I'm sorry, Ryun," I told him. "I'm really, really sorry."

And just like that, I turned and walked away, out of Ryun's life.

Epilogue

Since then Sierra and I have talked a little more.

And while we're not *best* friends and probably never will be again, I think we're pretty much okay now. She told me that she's been trying to forgive Ryun and me. But she also admitted that she doesn't have it completely figured out. I think that's because it's not one of those do-it-once-and-you're-done-with-it kinds of things.

The truth is, I'm still working on some forgiveness areas of my own.

It's been the easiest to forgive Sierra (for causing me to lose my job) since I realize she felt betrayed by me in the first place and just wanted to get even.

And I think I've almost forgiven Carin, since according to Sierra, Carin honestly believed that I was doing drugs and all that. I'm sure Carin thought she was doing everyone at Little Lambs a big favor by turning me in. But I just wish she would have come to me first. At least we're actually speaking to each other now, although I wouldn't call us friends.

It wasn't that hard to forgive Holly because I know I must've seemed like a totally horrible person to her when I showed up for that Valentine's dinner. I guess I was.

But I'm having the hardest time forgiving *myself.* I mean, I don't see how I could've turned into such a total idiot in such a short period of time. It was like I went from zero to 60 on the Road to Stupidity. But according to the Bible, which I've been reading, we need to forgive ourselves in order to forgive others. So I'm working on that too.

I'm happy to say that I have my job at Little Lambs back. And the board even apologized to both my mom and me for not following up on the story before they took action. The kids were so happy to have me back with them, but not nearly as happy as I was to be there. And now I'm starting to save up for college again.

Anna and I are thinking about going to college together next fall. I hadn't realized that she was considering the University of Virginia too. But then I suppose I had my head in the clouds back then. Back when my temporary insanity first began.

I can't even begin to describe how good it feels to be back in my own life again. And to not be playing the game of betrayal anymore. I had no idea that wanting to date the perfect guy and be part of the elite crowd would cost me so much.

That I'd get trapped in a web of lies and pain. Now I know they weren't worth it. *Nothing* is worth the lies . . . and feeling separated from God. At last I'm back in his company, and I never want to leave again.

degrees OF betrayal

Betrayal comes naturally—
where you stand will determine
who's to blame—but there's always
more than one side to the story.

sierra's story
{DANDI DALEY MACKALL}

ryun's story
{JEFF NESBIT}

kenzie's story
{MELODY CARLSON}

**For more insider info,
go to Degreesofbetrayal.com
and enter code betrayal03.**

A Sneak Peek at *Sierra's Story* ...

I'm trying so hard to remember that my head is splitting into pieces. I see white specks in the black, like tiny bone fragments. Who was with me? Not Ryun. *Please, God, not Ryun.*

But I can see myself behind the giant wheel of the old Chevy. I'm driving–to a football game. The last one of the season. I pick up Kenzie. And I know I'm driving to Ryun's.

Somebody tell me! Where are they? Are they okay? If I hurt them, I don't want to live. Is that why the police are here? I hurt McKenzie and Ryun? Did I kill them? Did I?

The room feels empty now. I want to scream for the police to come back so I can confess. *Yes! I did it! I don't remember, but I must have done this.* They won't believe me if I tell them I can't remember anything.

Not that I care if they believe me or not. It doesn't matter.

If I can ever talk again, I'll cry out so loud the whole state will hear me: "Yes! I did it. Bring on the judge. Bring on the gas pellets or the lethal needle. Take your pick. I don't care. Just let it be over."

Life, I mean. It might as well be.

■   ■   ■

"Hi, guys," I say, hoping I'm smiling warmly at both of them. Ryun's cheeks are red from the cold outside or the warmth of the hospital.

"We wanted to see how you're doing," Ryun says, not looking at me.

"Take off your coats," I urge.

"We can't stay," Kenzie says.

Ryun nods at her, then explains, "Yeah. I need to get to work."

Kenzie smiles. "You look good."

Ryun comes to my bed and kisses the top of my head. "Sorry we can't stay and talk and stuff." His gaze darts around the room.

Kenzie looks nervous.

They're making *me* nervous. Part of me wants them to leave. But that doesn't make sense. I hate it when they're not here. I'm so mixed-up. I feel like screaming.

Kenzie tugs Ryun's arm, as if to pull him toward the door.

The gesture jars me. Ice water shoots through my spine.

And just that fast, I know that I'm right. My best friend and my boyfriend. I'm on the wrong end of a country-western song.

"We should go," she says. And the *we* means something, something huge, something unfair.

Ryun looks at her the way he used to look at me—expectant, familiar. What they have isn't friendship. It's more than friendship. I can see that.

They leave, and I imagine them walking out of the hospital, their arms around each other. I picture them getting into Ryun's car. He opens the door. She slides in. He helps her fasten her seat belt. The engine starts. They're off on a romantic sunset drive together.

Or maybe not. Maybe they're going out for burgers at Riley's. I speed up the image, making them go faster and faster, pressing Ryun's foot to the floor. Kenzie reaches for his arm again, just like she did in my hospital room. Only now I imagine Ryun, jerking his hand away, shocked at Kenzie's move. The car drifts off the road. He pulls it back, but it's too sharp. The car flips over.

And *bang!* Missouri and I have two new roommates.

That part about the car flipping? I'm wondering if that's my subconscious trying to work its way up. Because the car I'm picturing isn't Ryun's car. It's the Chevy. Dad's '57 Chevy. And the sign in the background isn't Riley's. It's Route 58, where Officer McCarthy said the car went off the road. The scene of the accident.

A Sneak Peek at *Ryun's Story* . . .

I am invincible.

You don't believe me? Really? Well, watch this.

There used to be a straight road, about a quarter
of a mile long, out near the airport. It was behind
a couple of big warehouses. If the word got around,
and you heard about it, you could watch two kids
racing their cars just as it was getting dark.

They'd hit 120 mph or so, hope they didn't slide
or fishtail at the end, and then get out of there before
the cops could catch them. Every so often, a kid
would roll, get mangled, and die or something.

Then the cops started hanging around, waiting.
The city put up speed bumps. Finally they cut the
road in half.

But beneath that road is a huge empty water pipe.
I don't know what it was used for. Maybe carrying

sludge from one of the factories to a stagnant pond at the other end.

But now the factory's gone, and the pond is only dirt and trash. There's nothing at either end of this long straight pipe. It simply sits there. Waiting quietly, never complaining.

The pipe is just big enough for someone tall, like me, to walk through. I'm 6'2", taller than almost every other kid at Highview. I can walk through that pipe and my straight black hair doesn't even come close to touching the top. When I spread my arms wide, they barely touch either side. If you shout at one end, your voice disappears at the other.

I don't ever walk through that pipe, though. No, I leave an old Yamaha motorcycle out there, and I ride whenever I feel like it. I don't wear a helmet. I don't need to. I never wear a seat belt in a car either . . . I told you—nothing touches me. I always come out on top.

Anyway, the old Yamaha is one of those sport bikes where you have to ride low, your head down. I got it from one of my friends I play soccer with— a lawyer—who was bored with it. I picked up a little extra cash from my folks to pay for it.

They don't know I own it. My folks, I mean. There's a lot they don't know, actually. There's a lot *everyone* doesn't know . . . well, maybe except for my little sister, Joon, but she'd never give me up.

Here's how it works. You start at one end of the tunnel on the bike, get going, no lights. Then you kick into another gear. The bike jolts forward a little.

You put your head down lower. The light starts to dim. It gets darker.

Then you hit a time—maybe just a few seconds, maybe forever—when it's pitch dark. There's only the sound of the bike coming off the walls of the tunnel to guide you. You hope the bike is going straight, but you don't really know. You aim at the tiny dot of light at the other end of the tunnel and hope you have it right. Maybe you do—maybe you don't.

But I always have it right. I always hit that spot of light at the other end of the tunnel. The bike doesn't wobble or pitch. I don't ever have to adjust. I just aim and ride through the darkness. And I hit it perfectly every time.

It's such a rush. Light to dark to light. Fast to faster. And then—you *rip* out the other end into the brilliant light, going at least 80 or 90 mph across the dirt toward a line of trees. Plenty of time to stop the bike.

I can do it 100 times, a million times. I never get tired of the feeling. There's a point where you can't be afraid, because you know that if you are, you'll lose it. The bike will roll or tilt, and it will all end. Your life, I mean. But when you know you're invincible, you're not afraid. You just go, as fast as you can, until you blast out the other end.

It's funny what happens when you live your life this way, as if you're untouchable. When I'm on a soccer field, there are times when I *know* I cannot be stopped. There may be one or two—or even three—defenders in my way. But I simply go around them, through them. I carry the ball with me as I go, and then I put the ball near post, upper 90, wherever it needs to be.

I've never told this to anyone. I'm not sure anyone would understand it or even believe it. I'm not sure anyone would even care. It isn't an easy thing to explain.

We all die some day. I know that. But not me right now, not this way. I am invincible. I can do what I want, when I want. It's just the way it is.

About the Author

Melody Carlson is the award-winning author of more than 90 books for children, teens, and adults—with sales totaling more than two million. In addition to *Kenzie's Story,* her young adult best-sellers include *Miranda's Story* in the Degrees of Guilt series for teens (Tyndale) and the Diary of a Teenage Girl series (Multnomah), which has received great reviews and a large box of fan mail, as well as *Looking for Cassandra Jane* (Tyndale), *Finding Alice* (Waterbrook), and an exciting new teen series called TrueColors (NavPress).

Over the years Melody Carlson has worn many hats—from preschool teacher to youth counselor to political activist to senior editor. But most of all, she *loves to write!* Currently she freelances from her home. Melody and her husband, Chris, who now have two grown sons, have always had a great heart for teens—they met twenty-five years ago as Young Life counselors. For a number of years they took troubled teens into their home.

Melody and Chris live in central Oregon with their chocolate Lab retriever. They enjoy skiing, hiking, gardening, camping, and biking in the beautiful Cascade Mountains.

areUthirsty.com

Degreesofbetrayal.com

degrees

guilt

Sammy's dead...they each played a par
Kyra, his twin sister. Miranda, the girl
loved. And Tyrone, a friend from schoo

WHAT'S THE REAL STORY

**There's always more than
one point of view—read all three.**

kyra's story
{DANDI DALEY MACKALL}
ISBN 0-8423-8284-4

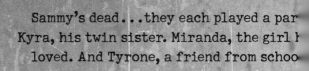

miranda's story
{MELODY CARLSON}
ISBN 0-8423-8283-6

tyrone's story
{SIGMUND BROUWER}
ISBN 0-8423-8285-2

degreesofguilt.c

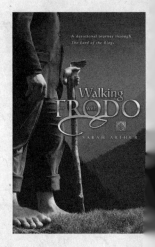

New from Sarah Arthur

COMING 2005

WALKING WITH

Bilbo

continue the journey. . .

If you ever need a shoulder to cry on or a hand to hold, mine can reach all the way across the world.

best friends
an ocean apart
surviving life together

Hands across the

MOON

jane g. meyer

Life isn't what best friends Gretchen and Mia had in mind. They'd looked forward to their junior year together—in California. Then Gretchen had to move to Ecuador . . . a world away. Now, nothing's going right for either of them.

Sometimes it seems that their "across the moon" letters are their best lifeline.

areUthirsty.com

ISBN 0-8423-8286-0